A Gathering Misery

A Clemenceau's Daughters Novel
Book 2

Rocky Porch Moore

Published by:
Southern Yellow Pine (SYP) Publishing
4351 Natural Bridge Rd.
Tallahassee, FL 32305

www.syppublishing.com

This is a work of fiction. Names, characters, places, and events that occur either are the products of the author's imagination or are used fictitiously. Any resemblance to actual persons, places, or events is purely coincidental.

The contents and opinions expressed in this book do not necessarily reflect the views and opinions of Southern Yellow Pine Publishing, nor does the mention of brands or trade names constitute endorsement.

ISBN-10: 1-59616-061-6
ISBN-13: 978-1-59616-061-3
ISBN-13: ePub 978-1-59616-062-0
ISBN-13: Adobe PDF 978-1-59616-063-7
Library of Congress Control Number: 2018939543

Printed in the United States of America
First Edition
March 2018

In memory of Linda

Acknowledgements

This is a work of fiction. It is not a memoir. The setting, in part, however, is very much autobiographical and reflects the places of my childhood as accurately as memory, and the psyche of a precocious character, which I attempt to capture, allow. The characters and events are my inventions and do not directly parallel relationships I experienced, but rather reflect the tendency of the past to cling to the present, both personally and societally. The family saga belongs to the characters; it is not my own.

I would like to thank Terri Gerrell and Southern Yellow Pine Publishing for helping me bring this story to fruition. I thank the Florida Authors and Publishers Association for providing continual coaching and support throughout the process. I also thank John Fleming of Publisher.Cloud for his invaluable know-how and guidance in media presence and marketing.

Finally, thanks to Russ Moore for his love and support throughout this grand adventure.

Prologue

What mother hasn't bargained with man, the devil, or even God himself to make a way for her child? What mother hasn't offered her own soul in exchange for the safekeeping of her beloved? What mother hasn't, at some point, second-guessed the wisdom in such an offer when the child eventually, as she must, disappoints or betrays the trust of that indelible bond? The umbilical cord is cut at birth, forever separating one into two. At its best, it's the inverse of a marriage. That union, in the eyes of God and man, joins two into one, until death do they part. The product of that union becomes a lasting manifestation of the blessed state… or the damned state, accordingly.

Part One

Daughter

Alabama, 198-

1

Deborah

It was a lost season. Deborah Ballard, her hair shorn in grief, sat on the half-rotten porch swing that hung listlessly beneath the arm of an ancient, knotty oak. In between the whoosh of cars punctuated by the roar of an occasional 18 wheeler, she could hear the gentle clacking of the twigs high in the tree. The twigs carried the lifeblood of the oak, reaching upward toward the warmth of the sun and entangling their fingers in the effort to rise. What little breeze there was did not reach her as she sat shrouded beneath the canopy of green.

Just as the twigs of the oak were clamoring for precious sunlight, the fingerling roots dug in a different direction. Downward they stretched, as relentless in their pursuit of loamy darkness as the light-craving twigs spanning high above. In this subterranean crepuscule, the oak finds its might. Growth is a synthesis of multidirectional cynosure; in order for the tree to stand tall, it must divide its strength. It must divide its focus. It must divide its trust. If the oak spends all its time reaching for the sun, it will be easily toppled by storms that will come as surely as the rain. If the oak spends all its energy searching the depths, it will wither and crumble from within. Either way, it's a matter of time, and time is an expert at waiting.

The swing creaks as Deborah sighs and shifts to hug her knees to her chest. She feels the slats bend and strain with her weight even though she's nothing but a runt of a thirteen-year-old. She wonders which will rot first: the seat of the wooden swing or the hemp that ties it to the tree. She wonders who will pick it up when it falls. Who will repair it? The twigs above seem to respond, but their answer is swept away by the mechanical strain of a downshifting truck as it powers beyond the hillcrest where Nonny's driveway meets the busy county road. She already knows the answer anyway.

"Little Debbie?" Nonny calls from the front door, nothing but her head sticking out between the utilitarian brick and the equally unwelcoming painted door. Actually, the door was partially painted. The bottom third of the door was a faded red, brushstrokes visible and rising unevenly toward eye level. The rest of the door was a sickly green, pale and milky. High up on the door were three, tiny diamond-shaped windows of fogged glass. Only a very tall man would be able to see out of those windows if a visitor knocked, and what he could see would be distorted by the water-streaked glass. Where a doorbell should have been, a hand printed sign made from the stirring stick of a gallon of paint stood guard, haphazardly screwed into the doorframe. It read "No Solisiting." The misspelling rankled Deborah every time she entered through the front door, just like Nonny's insistence on calling her Little Debbie even though way too much had happened for such a cutesy name to fit. Nonny didn't seem to mind it a bit. When Deborah pointed out the error almost immediately upon her arrival, Nonny told her to hush up and mind her own business. As for her name, Nonny said Deborah was too much name for a shaggy-headed girl, and she'd call her what she damn well pleased in her own house, seeing as how she'd taken her to raise now. Deborah tucked that insult away, swallowing it down hard, mainly because it had just enough truth in it to burn on the way down. She'd take it, but Nonny couldn't make her go back to being someone she could never be again, not really.

"Little Debbie!" Nonny called again. "You git on in here. It's time we go see your Papa." Nonny already had that odd plastic bonnet tied on her head. Old women wore them to protect their hair from rain or wind after they'd had it set at the beauty

2

parlor before Sunday meeting. Nonny had a standing appointment at Mrs. Garlan's garage-turned-shoppe just across the highway. Deborah walked Nonny there at nine a.m. on Saturday mornings—and not a minute earlier because punctuality is next to Godliness—and sat on the rusted metal glider placed out in front of the garage door so folks would know it wasn't a really a garage but a place of business. Next to her sat a largely unread copy of the King James Bible which Nonny constantly pressed on her.

She wasn't allowed to sit inside the parlor, even on those early cold days with Nonny when the mercurial Alabama winter gasped out its final breaths. She would say good morning to Mrs. Garlan as the heavily made up hairdresser helped Nonny to the sink chair. Either the lighting of the makeshift parlor or the heavy-handiness of the application made Mrs. Garlan appear clownish, grotesque even. Mrs. Garlan clucked disapprovingly and made some remark about her being a pitiful tow-headed goose, and Deborah left her grandmother in Mrs. Garlan's expert hands.

Never was there an offer to trim Deborah's choppy bob into a more pleasing shape. Mrs. Garlan was a widow-woman just like Nonny, and what they had to say to each other was "none of your business, Little Debbie." So, she waited for the two hours it took to shampoo, dry, and wrestle Nonny's hair into the teased and shellacked bun that was her one outward expression of vanity, saved expressly for rejoicing in the Lord come Sunday morning.

"C'mon, gal! Quit your lollygagging!" Nonny scolded as Deborah hurried across the front yard to meet Nonny in the carport. She heard the deadbolt slide on the front door and outpaced Nonny as she made her way to the head of the stairs at the back door, which was really on the side of the house. There was no exit from the house into the backyard whatsoever.

At school, when the fire chief came to scare the bee-Jesus out of all the kids at the annual "You're all going to burn your house down with your circuit-popping trees and die in your beds

3

before we can get to you and how's that for a Merry Christmas" speech, she had at first been dazzled by his resplendent uniform, brass buttons alight in the spotlight glow of the auditorium. He announced with just enough jocularity in his tone that most fires start in either the kitchen or the living room. He tried to hide his excitement, but that tiny upswing in his voice gave him away: he wanted someone's house to burn down. Reading people was even more fun than reading books, especially when they showed their secrets. It was more than secrets, though. Deborah wanted to know. She wanted to know that, statistically, kids who sleep in the top berth of bunkbeds are goners in a house fire. She wanted to know better than to wake up dead.

That was the right word for it, jocularity. She looked it up in the teacher's dictionary while she was studying for the spelling bee before the assembly. What was the point in spelling a word if you don't know how to use it? Deborah, on account of being so smart, was allowed to use the "real" dictionary that Miss Kinsee kept on her private shelf behind her desk. She also kept a tattered photo of a little boy who shared her bulbous nose taped to the pull-out part of her desk where nobody could see it. Deborah discovered it when Miss Kinsee stepped out of the room to go to the mimeograph machine. She was supposed to be gathering up the erasers for beating against the back wall of the school building but couldn't resist the opportunity to explore when she found herself suddenly alone in the classroom.

Deborah just wanted to know what sorts of things a teacher kept inside her desk. There was no harm in that. She needed to know in case she decided to become one someday. Besides, everybody has secrets squirreled away. All she did was collect them and save them up in case she needed them some time in the future. Miss Kinsee was not married. That's why she was a Miss. So, how did she have a son, and why had she never mentioned him to the class?

Deborah didn't really go looking for secrets unless the hunt simply fell in her lap, like the sweet serendipity of Miss Kinsee

4

leaving the classroom. Serendipity was another one of the spelling words. It meant luck or even happiness finding you without you even having to try. She knew now, however, that those unlooked-for fortunes were meant for other girls. Serendipity doesn't come to girls who killed their brother. That's why Mom sent her away. That's why Deputy Barnevelder pitched the go-cart over the side of July Mountain. That's why Daddy didn't save her, wouldn't even look her in the eye. That's why she's with Nonny now. So what if the only exits at Nonny's house are through the two most fire-prone areas? She deserves misery.

Deborah helped Nonny down the steps, her ancient-looking, creepy alligator hide pocketbook clutched in her hand as if the secrets of the world were tucked inside. The purse latched with the Paleozoic feet of some poor dead baby alligator who had suffered the injustice of having snaps fused to its severed soles. It smelled musty, like aged sweat mixed with talcum powder. In fact, the pocketbook suited Nonny to a T.

"You can never be too careful around stairs, Little Debbie," began Nonny as if it were the first time the thought occurred to her even though Deborah practically had the Stairs Speech memorized. She had been surprised when Nonny launched into it the second Saturday on the way to the cemetery and perplexed the third. That's before she learned about patterns. "People die on stairs. An old widow-woman like me could fall and break her hip. Then she might as well be dead. If the fall don't do it, catching pneumonia in the hospital while she's healing up will. If it don't, why then she's no use to herself and will wind up in the nursing home with some stranger wiping her ass. Little Debbie, if I fall down these stairs and break my hip, I want you to take that hammer hanging on the nail by the door and bash my brains out. You've made it happen before, and you can do it again if you need to. It'd be a mercy and a thank you for me taking you on and raising you while your mother works through her grieving. Now, let's go on to the cemetery and see your Papa."

5

2

Deborah

Deborah helped Nonny work her way down into the passenger seat of Levin's New Yorker, as Nonny called it. The car was so long its tail end was left exposed to the Alabama sun and the runoff from the carport roof. With the exception of the faded, rain-beaten strip on the trunk, it was just the color of the wings of a Junebug. Its roof, in contrast, was stark white. Nonny was clearly proud of this car, Papa's last major purchase on this side of Heaven, and pointed out that "Levin selected the color to please me, since it clearly matches my wall-to-wall carpeting." Deborah found it wholly old and unappealing, much like Nonny's ugly carpet..., much like Nonny.

Deborah walked around to the driver's side and slid in behind the wheel even though she knew she had no business driving and would probably go to jail if the police noticed enough to stop them while they were on the highway. She was nowhere near old enough to have a license, or even to want one for that matter, but Nonny insisted on being chauffeured to the grocery store, church, and the cemetery on account of her being an old widow woman and it not being proper for her to have to drive herself around. So Deborah sat propped up on a pair of old football cushions that read "Go Knights" in faded yellow letters and made involuntary fart sounds every time Deborah shifted her weight. For some reason, the cushions reminded her of Brent. She almost smiled thinking of how he would have cut up to hear those cushions toot and try to place the blame on Nonny.

Deborah noticed that no other young people seemed to be driving their widowed grandparents places, but Nonny appeared to be oblivious to the rules of the outside world. She operated on her own sense of propriety, which, as far as Deborah could tell, made about as much sense as putting a screen door on a submarine. Besides, it didn't take long for her to learn that there was just no arguing with Nonny. Deborah figured this was why Mom kept a wide berth, and it became clear pretty quickly that maybe July Mountain wasn't quite far enough away from Nonny's reach.

Deborah navigated onto Rescue Road where Papa and a bunch of other dead relatives she didn't know were planted in a naked, treeless field just across the road from a church that had seen better days. She parked the Chrysler on the gravel parking lot that occupied the front yard of the church. Not so much as a privet hedge separated the parking area from the whitewashed door with the word Sanctuary neatly hand-printed in black.

"Just pull right up there to the door, Little Debbie," instructed Nonny. "You ain't gonna block nobody today, and I'll be damned if we don't take the good spot while the getting's good."

Nonny got out of the Chrysler with ease and fairly trotted as she crossed Rescue Road without even a glance for traffic. She could be fit and spry or a pitiful old woman, whichever served her purpose at the moment. "Nonny," Deborah called, "you didn't even look before you crossed the street!"

"Child, even God ain't got a cruel enough sense of humor to lay me low while I'm crossing the road to talk to Levin. Oh, no. He's got other plans for me, and for you, too, Missy." Nonny called Deborah Missy whenever she suspected sass. She heard teachers at school call girls Missy, too, when they were back-talking, but only Nonny thought poorly enough of Deborah to call her that name, and only Nonny said it with such a tone of disgust that it made Deborah feel guilty whether she was or not.

Someone had embedded a set of concrete steps on the ditch bank, the kind folks sometimes put in front of trailer doors when they don't have the wherewithal to put up a proper deck. The steps were cracked from the top down, right down the middle. Deborah thought of that part in the Bible where the Lord rent the curtain at the temple in half right at the moment Jesus keeled over on the cross. It was like He'd opened up the pathway from Heaven down to earth so folks could just holler straight up to Him instead of having to ask the preacher to do it for them.

Deborah didn't really understand why people had to use Sadducees and Pharisees and such to talk to God back in the Bible days, but the King James Bible Nonny made her spend unending hours with seemed to point that way. It was hard to tell with all the thees, thous, and begets, but the Word of the Lord kind of grew on her after she'd given up on fighting Nonny and just let the reading happen. She remembered loving a set of Bible storybooks when she was little. The memory of those books brought back a flood of images surrounding the green house in Woods Cove... Fat Sarah's sweet singing and hard eyes; the exposed and tangled roots of the oak tree, dripping clay like blood clots after the tornado struck; the body of GodLutherYouStink, the dog with an unforgettable name and an odor she'd recognize even now; the steps where Grandpa met the Lord.

Nonny mumbled something unintelligible that brought Deborah out of her reverie and had her scrambling up the split steps to enter the graveyard proper. The steps were the only thing that marked an entrance to the graveyard. No fence or trees lined it. The headstones stood erect in straight lines, not quite parallel to Rescue Road. Deborah noticed this the first time she brought Nonny here to talk. Although the gravesites were neat and trim, the entire graveyard was out of kilter. It was as if whoever set the plumb line for the headstones was off the mark just a tad. It was off-putting and Deborah said so.

8

"Don't you speak ill of the dead, Missy!" chastised Nonny. "Most of 'em's been dead longer than you've been alive, so they know a thing or two about how they lie resting. Besides, the graveyard was here well before Rescue Road got laid, so I'm betting it's the road that is cockeyed and not the graveyard."

Nonny made a beeline for the center of the graveyard, which was where all the family awaited the trumpet call that would make the dead arise and ride on a cloud behind Jesus all the way to Heaven. Deborah figured that made Jesus a sort of glorified bus driver and tried to imagine Him honking the horn on a giant cloud-bus to wake up the dead folks. It didn't seem very God-like to have to haul a world's worth of people, living, dead, or dry rotted away to nothing, all the way to Heaven. What it seemed like was hard work. Wouldn't it be easier for God and Jesus to just set up house down on Earth?

Thinking of that imaginary cloud-bus got Deborah to thinking about black folks and worrying over whether the ones who died before they could ride anywhere they damn well pleased on the bus would know they didn't have to move to the back. She didn't have any problem with who sat where on a bus and didn't really see where the color of skin made a hill of beans in the case. All the same, she had enough sense not to reveal that she had sat beside a milk chocolate-colored girl with tiny braids sticking out all over her head all the way to Montgomery on the fourth-grade field trip to see the state capitol. She was the odd child out, and the teacher asked Debbie special to ride beside the shy girl because Debbie was "growed up enough to know they ain't no cooties on 'em." Her pride outweighed her common sense, and she didn't think Daddy would know the difference so she agreed. The teacher, however, picked a pair of boys to sit together on the return trip just to be fair.

"Deborah! Quit daydreaming and come help me over here," Nonny called.

Nonny knelt down beside the headstone that read "Levin Walker Clemm 1907-1978 At Rest in Jesus," her craggy knuckles clutching the granite for support. Deborah thought Nonny was about to start praying, but her free hand plucked the volunteer dill weed growing next to the stone, uprooting it and tossing it aside. She tamped down the ground where she uprooted the weeds so the grave didn't look pocked.

Deborah got on her hands and knees and began to crawl across to get to the weeds sprouting out of Nonny's reach on the far side of the headstone. "Don't you get on that grave. It's disrespectful and dangerous. Go around the other side of the stone to get at those weeds." Butted up on the backside of Papa's marker was another marker, an L.R. Leederman who must have really liked racecars since there was one engraved on his stone. Still on her knees, Deborah crawled a respectable distance around L.R. to circle back to the task at hand.

"What the devil are you doing crawling clear down there?" Nonny had her head up over the stones. Her sizable rump stuck out to the side and she looked for all the world like her head had been separated from her body. That odd plastic hairdo protector glinted in the sunlight and created a halo effect about her head, which only added to the impression.

"I'm crawling around this grave like you said," Deborah replied plaintively.

"Don't be a damn fool. It's your own family you don't disrespect by wallowing on their graves."

"Oh," said Deborah and just crawled around faster. Keeping up with all the rules for family conduct was ponderous, indeed, and had not gotten any simpler since she started living at Nonny's house. It was like she was expected to know all of the rules automatically and to know that those rules only applied in certain situations. It wasn't like a formula where you did the same thing every time. She just couldn't seem to get it right. Deborah cleared out the rest of the dill weed, being careful not to put too much weight on her grandfather's grave.

Nonny unlatched the alligator feet that held her pocketbook secure and brought out a small bottle of whisky like one of those

10

they have in fancy hotels on TV shows. She sprinkled the amber liquid across Papa's grave. "There's your snort, Levin. I wouldn't let you have it in life, but I ain't going to deny you in the hereafter. So, you remember that, and just keep yourself put down there in that grave where you belong. Don't you come wandering back up to the house at night rifling through the closets and looking at me lying in our bed. I ain't asleep, and I see you. You ain't going to have to guzzle down no more cough syrup. I got your snort right here. You just stay put, now."

The hairs rose up on Deborah's arms. Nonny was talking to that headstone like it was a sounding board. "I've brought your granddaughter, the one who got your head busted up so you could meet Jesus. If you hadn't been trying to make it up to your own daughter, you'd still be here. You always told me to just let the past lie right there in the past because it's not any use anymore. You know you was wrong about that now, don't you?"

"Nonny?" Deborah placed her hand on Nonny's shoulder, and Nonny's head shot up like she'd been caught whispering in church. She sloughed off Deborah's hand.

"Hush, child. Can't you see I'm talking? Go on over there a piece while I finish up. Go find some of the babies. Their headstones have little lambs engraved right on them."

Deborah was far less interested in rooting out dead babies in the cemetery than she was in hearing what Nonny had to say to a long dead grandpa. She thought Nonny should've made her peace years ago. Debbie hadn't even started school when Papa died in her backyard. She barely remembered it, and if she were truthful, she barely remembered him. Mom kept a single photo of him buried deep in her wallet, and the main thing Deborah remembered was an incident that had little to do with him and more to do with Mom.

***

11

It was summer and Mom loaded up the car with a couple of rods and reels and a picnic basket. Deborah rode shotgun while Brent slid around on the vinyl backseat getting to have more fun as usual. Mom avoided Daddy's tackle store and instead stopped by the old bait shop for a container of worms. She said she just wanted to fish without having to go through umpteen lessons on how to do it properly. She didn't understand why folks, and by folks she meant Daddy, tried to take all the fun out of fishing with a bunch of scientifically proven gadgetry. A worm dangling on a hook gave a fish a fighting chance. It could choose whether it was hungry without being mesmerized by some shiny geehaw. She didn't see the sport in taking advantage of the fish or taking the work out of the fishing. That's what was wrong with the world these days: folks take the mystery out of everything; and when they take away the mystery, they take away the fun.

They were off to the city-maintained park where picnic tables sat right by the side of the lake, shade trees held the Alabama heat at bay, and the breeze off the water made the thick air move in lazy eddies that Deborah could almost see. A steady stream of rednecks cruised the park circle at a walking pace so drivers could admire the water and the parade of bass boats dotting the lake. It was a picture-perfect moment. Peanut butter and jelly sandwiches that Mom made the good way—with the peanut butter and jelly mixed up in a bowl before getting spread on loaf bread so the jelly wouldn't soak through and make the bread soggy—were wrapped in waxed paper and waiting in the basket next to a giant bag of potato chips. Mom had even bought them a round of ice-cold bottled Cokes at the bait shop to wash it all down. It would be a fine morning out by the lake.

Aside from the tacit air of disapproval that Mom breathed in like fine perfume as she took the children out of bounds, Daddy was absent from this memory. Deborah couldn't remember anything being amiss. He just wasn't part of this family moment. Mom even laughed when Brent's first cast sent the worm flying off the hook in an arc before it hit the water. She showed the

12

children how to bait the hook properly and admonished them to be extra careful not to hook themselves. She told a brief but terrifying story about fishhooks having to be removed from hands and fingers with a pair of pliers at the emergency room. She ensured Deborah's careful attention to detail with the fact that a visit to the emergency room would include a tetanus shot so the fishhook wouldn't "give us all lockjaw." Deborah was old enough now to know that lockjaw isn't contagious, but back then, the threat of a tetanus shot was enough to keep both children extra-vigilant as they fished for crappie, bream, or whatever fish would be unlucky enough to hit the hook.

Mom and Deborah were munching chips when a car door slammed shut behind them and the driver gunned it, throwing gravel as the car sped out of the park. "Crazy kids," Mom laughed. Then, everything changed.

Suddenly Mom was screaming, "My purse! My purse!" The happiness of the moment drained as quickly as pulling the plug on a bathtub. Brent's practice cast flew backwards in reaction to Mom's shriek, catching the line in the tree. Deborah grabbed the rod from Brent to shake the line loose just as Mom spun around to yell at the kids to load up immediately. The next thing Deborah knew, Mom wrestled the rod from her hands, knocking her down in the process. Mom was crying, cussing a blue streak, and fighting that tree as if it were Lucifer himself. "Get up and get the scissors!" Mom hollered at Deborah. Brent was already in full retreat to the car.

Deborah dashed to the car to grab the scissors that Mom kept in the glove compartment just in case. She had scissors squirreled away all over the place because she never could find a pair when she needed them. Deb ran the scissors back to Mom with little regard for scissor safety. As many times as she'd heard about not running with scissors, it didn't seem to matter when your mother was in a tizzy. Mom cut the line, leaving it hanging from the tree and high-tailed it to the car. Deb was right on her heels because she didn't want to get left.

13

Of course, by this time, the carload of young thieves was already long gone, but Mom caught gravel herself as she whipped their hatchback into pursuit. Brent slid across the vinyl bench of the backseat as she took the park lane curves at breakneck speed.

"Mom!" cried Deb as she held onto the dashboard to steady herself. "Mommy!" Her own screech seemed to snap Mom out of her rage. She pulled the car over and leveled her eyes at Deb.

"We could've caught them if you hadn't gotten the line tangled up. I ought to take that rod to your ass." Deb covered her incredulity quickly and lowered her eyes. Even Brent had enough sense to keep his mouth shut. Mom let out a deep breath and pulled back onto the road. All of the anger just blew right out of her as she looked in the rearview mirror and said, "Well, Brent, it's your lucky day. We were going to have lunch at the Burger Chef, but now we'll just have your favorite hotdogs at home. I'm worn out."

The shortest route home involved driving by the town dump, which stank to high heaven. They didn't normally take the shortcut because of the smell and Daddy's proclamation that they should drive the extra five minutes around the dump to avoid having to look at all the trash living in run-down trailers and houses that weren't much more than plywood and cardboard. It was up by the dump where the mixed folks lived, colored and whites together. Daddy said there wasn't anything worse than a white woman taking up with a black man. It was the deepest kind of shame. "I'd forgive you almost anything, Little Debbie, but never that. You'd never set foot in my house again. Don't you forget it."

They topped the hill by the dump, driving slowly because children, all willy-nilly, black, white, and in between, were playing in the ditch on the side of the road. The houses were so close to the blacktop Mom was practically driving through their front yards. Nobody had fences, and hardly anybody had grass. "Ain't a Mama in sight looking after these young'uns," said Mom. "It's a wonder they don't all get run over, what with the

14

garbage trucks riding this road all the time. Would you look at that? I don't believe it!" Deb thought Mom had seen some kid lying out in the middle of the road when Mom braked hard enough to make Deb have to put her arm out to keep from hitting the dashboard. Brent thumped hard against the seat backs as Mom skidded to a stop, jumping out of the car at a dead run.

Hanging on the City Dump sign was a purse, Mom's purse! Mom yanked it off the sign and was digging in it before she could get back into the car good. "My driver's license, insurance card: it's all here! Cash is gone, but there weren't but ten dollars anyway." Then Mom started laughing so hard tears poured out of her eyes. "They Lord!" she exclaimed. "They took my pills! What on earth would boys want with birth control pills?" Mom was sure enough tickled, but then she got serious.

"Kids, get out of the car. We've got to pray. C'mon, now!" Mom marched Deb and Brent back over to that City Dump sign and got down on her knees right there in front of God, a mountain of garbage, and a passel of kids who'd come up out of the ditch to see what was happening. "Get down and bow your heads!" Deb bowed her head, but looked out of the corner of her eyes at her mama praying like a madwoman for the miracle of driving by the dump and finding her pocketbook. It was the first time she'd heard Mom pray out loud. Instead of prayer being a balm, like that friendly Vacation Bible School teacher said, the prayer had a disquieting effect on Deb. When they got up, the unwatched children scattered back across the ditch, and Deb felt ashamed to be seen next to a mama who would pray at a dump. Mom must have felt the awkward abashment as well because she ordered Deb and Brent not to mention the theft, the miracle, or especially the praying to Daddy. "If you do, I'll take every last one of your toys and burn them on the brush pile." She meant it, too.

***

15

It was hard to think about Mom without the sadness about Brent's accident bubbling up and threatening to overtake Deborah, how she failed to save her brother, and in that failure lost Brent, Mom, and Daddy all in a single afternoon. She also lost school. When Nonny took her, it was like school just no longer existed. That was fine for a while as she was too distraught to think about much of anything. Now, as the summer dragged on, she wondered if and where she would go to school. Nonny made no mention of it, and if she learned anything at all with her time with Nonny, it was that you don't go asking for things you want. Nonny was funny that way.

Deborah could no longer hear Nonny's graveside muttering as she wove her way through the headstones, doing the math on the ones whose families didn't kindly provide the number of years spent here on earth before crossing that bridge into the hereafter. She almost chuckled at some of the old-fashioned names—Beulah, Winnifred, Augustus—and did titter at some poor toddler forever remembered as "Little Stinky." There were several markers that indicated a grave shared by a mother and her baby. These were the saddest, all that hope tamped down in a grave. Deborah wondered if there was a little baby casket down there in addition to the mama's casket. Maybe the miniature casket was tucked inside the larger one so that the bones wouldn't get mixed up. Maybe the baby was just placed in the mama's arms so she could hold it forevermore. She wanted to know if gravediggers charge per grave or by the person.

Deborah was now in the far corner of the cemetery, in what looked to be its oldest part. Here, the markers were untended, weedy. The engravings on the stones were weathered and tired-looking. Some of them were even askew as the ground around them had puckered and settled, fault lines evident in both the markers and the occasional concrete slabs that staked a final earthly claim. Here was a Horace, with three wives laid out beside him: two Anne's and an Aethel. It was hard to read the dates, but all three wives died in childbirth. Only Aethel had the

16

baby "infant son" with her. Deborah hoped the other children lived, but they would've died out by now. Maybe nobody was left to tend the old graves. Deborah got to work and weeded around the stones of Old Horace and his wives. As she pulled, she discovered that one of the Anne's, the one on the left, was "beloved." Beloved as she was, two other wives rested between her and Old Horace. Deborah wondered what she thought about that and whether they all got along in Heaven. She imagined the three wives strolling down a golden street, pushing the carriages of the babies who had killed them getting born, with Old Horace just a-grinning like the cat who ate the canary.

Just beyond Old Horace, a junk pile of beat-up wreaths and faded out fake flower sprays marked the boundary of the cemetery. Even though it was snaky, Deborah waded in and plucked out a couple of decorations that weren't worn slap dab out. She put a bouquet on Beloved Anne's marker because she felt sorry for her having to make way for two other wives. She placed a water-logged stuffed lamb toy at Aethel's spot for the nameless infant son. It rankled her that Old Horace didn't bother to name the baby. Maybe he just gave up.

Maybe that's what happened with Mom. When Brent got killed, she had her fill of dying and just gave up, but she gave up on me. She still had me, but she gave up anyway. I'll never forgive that. Deborah was surprised by the sudden venom she felt toward her mother and, by proxy, Old Horace. It rose like bile, and she hocked a wad of phlegm onto the headstone. "That's for giving up, you old bastard," she hissed. Immediately, she looked around to make sure Nonny remained out of earshot. No telling what Nonny would do if she heard Deborah use such a word. Nonny used damns and hells frequently, but it was a grievous sin for a girl to pepper her language with trashy talk.

Nonny was already across the road, leaning against the bumper of the Chrysler, waiting. Deborah hurried along, weaving through the headstones and jumping plots to avoid stepping on

17

graves. She was breathless when she reached Nonny but felt some better.

"Looks like you found plenty of folks to talk to, Little Debbie," Nonny said equably. "That's the thing about graveyards; they're great for clearing out what you got bottled up on the inside. Ain't nobody but you talking, but plenty of folks listening. The trick is to make sure those listening are dead."

3

Isom

Caro always went to bed well before he did, especially after she'd taken that ridiculously stupid three to eleven p.m. shift at the hospital. He couldn't make her understand that she didn't need to work; he was making enough money to keep them comfortable. In fact, he was on the cusp of becoming well-to-do. It was an embarrassment to him that she persisted in her nursing job. She called it a career like some sort of women's libber. Wiping asses and watching blips on a screen waiting on some old bag to finally die didn't seem like much of a career to him. As long as she had to make reports and kiss ass in addition to wiping it, it was just a job.

Now, he was his own man; made his own decisions. He built his tackle store from nothing. He expanded his reach until he was the sole proprietor of an entire shopping center—eight storefronts in all—with plans that would finally put tired, old Scottsboro on the map for something other than framing niggers. He was a true businessman, he thought with pride. Now, that's a career.

He needed sleep, but rest eluded Isom Ballard since the burial back in February. He sat on his dead son's bed nursing yet another beer. Caro had finally stripped it a couple of weeks ago, but she hadn't yet found the heart to re-make it. The space fighter sheets were gone; he had no idea where. Somehow, the piss-stained mattress was even more depressing than the juvenile bedding. Isom reached down between his legs, fingers searching for the hole in the box spring casing. He pulled out the revolver and brought it up to rest on his naked thigh. At first, he was worried Caro would learn his secret when she at last began to repurpose Brent's room. She couldn't stand to live in a shrine, she said. He wasn't sure he could stand not to.

Isom found himself in here nightly, taking note of Caro's systematic dismantling of Brent's earthly remains. For months, his room remained untouched. Dirty clothes, basketball shoes, and video game cartridges littered the floor. A single mud-caked football cleat lay in the corner up under his dresser. That crazy cow toy that needed its tail pumped so it would squirt chalk-water milk out its teat lay cockeyed against the window sash holding up the mini blind, udder shining as the crack of its tail/pump held enough louvers up to let the security light from the garage shine onto the head of the bed.

Clever, chicken-shit boy, he thought. Brent was always afraid of the dark. Isom thought he'd beaten it out of him. No Ballard boy of his would ever be a sissy. Isom caught himself grinning because Brent outfoxed him; but with the next beer, memory quickly turned to despair as he dissolved helplessly into self-loathing, a litany of crushed opportunities playing themselves out like a cruel looped reel. There was no Ballard boy at all anymore.

He shifted, and the cool of the steel reminded him of the revolver resting on his bare leg. He opened the chamber as he stood and crossed Brent's room, automatically picking his way through the maze of strewn clothes and toys no longer there, hadn't been there for weeks, to open the hall closet. Rummaging through the battery box, he found the bullet he'd hidden in there earlier. He'd only dared this much once before: the night after the funeral. He slipped it into the chamber as he silently padded back into Brent's room while his wife slept afloat—*How can she sleep?*—down the hall on the king-sized waterbed that might as well be an ocean away.

Isom sat back down on the barren twin bed and flicked his wrist to lock the chamber in place. He pictured himself in another time, the Old West, handling his pistol as naturally as if it were an extension of his hand. Caro took down all of Brent's posters except for an unsettling photo of Gopher from *The Love Boat*. Before, it was lost in a parade of sports heroes, superheroes, and *Star Wars* characters. Now it stood alone, the inexplicable sole survivor of Caro's slow-motion erasure of everything Brent.

He spun the cylinder and pressed the barrel deep in the hollow under his jaw. The first time he played this game with himself, the Devil, or God—*whatever difference that made*—he placed the barrel in his mouth. The taste of the metal was off-putting, and the idea of his teeth shattering with the blast made him lose his nerve. He hated the reverberation when he pulled the trigger and the pin snapped its judgment. The purser from *The Love Boat* grinned mockingly at him as his finger applied persistent pressure, waiting to feel that almost imperceptible point of no return when the gun married itself to firing. The sudden thought of Gopher's goofy-ass grin being the last thing he'd ever see made him avert his eyes.

The revolver clicked its decision.

Isom thought he saw a reflection in the window. He slugged down the last of the beer, skunky and warm in its crinkled can, and strode to the spot where that damned squirting cow used to stand guard over his dead chicken-shit son. The mini blind was still bent to let the light in. Something was taped to the bottom corner of the window frame back behind the blinds. As Ballard pushed the blinds aside with the barrel of the revolver, his first thought was that Brent hid a baseball card, but it wasn't a major league player depicted on the card. It was one of those cockamamie prayer cards like Catholics keep in their wallets to remind them they'll never match up to the suffering or glory of the Lord.

"By God, I've suffered," Isom sneered as the face of Jesus looked on in what could be nothing other than condescension. "Why'd you let it happen? Why'd you kill my boy?" He put the muzzle right up against the Jesus card and pulled the trigger.

Click.

21

Another failure.

Ballard looked closer. That card wasn't taped or tacked to the frame like a kid would do. It was one of those artsy glue jobs, decoupage. This was Caro's doing. Not only was she cleaning out poor Brent's room, she was trying to get the Lord's blessing. Well, Jesus didn't protect Brent when he was alive, so what the hell use would he be now? He tried to scratch the card off the wood, but his nails were nothing but nubs these days, and the gluing technique Caro used had the damn thing fused.

Pissed, he stalked down the hallway to confront her. Even sound asleep, Caro had a death grip on the frame of the bed. Her mortal fear of drowning kept her from venturing toward the center of the bed, for Christsakes. *"Stupid bitch,"* he thought as he watched her sleep. "You won't drown in this bed, darlin'," he slurred aloud. Her back was to him. She'd never even know what hit her.

Isom raised his gun, holding it just behind the back of her head. His hand shook a little, and he recognized he was good and drunk. He put his other hand on the butt of the revolver to steady himself. If he was going to do this, by God, he was going to do it right. He was sick of failing. A sharp intake of breath betrayed him as the chamber clicked once again, empty. Caro didn't even flinch, but a single tear escaped to slide in unseen silence down her cheek. Isom shrugged as casually as if he'd just missed church, turned, and headed back down the hall for another beer.

He put the revolver on the kitchen counter to rifle around the fridge for a fresh can, and the spell was broken. As he popped the top and the carbonated fizz expelled, it was like something popped the top on him and he found himself sobbing. He stood there in the glaring two a.m. spotlight of the refrigerator and cried for what he had become, for what he tried to do. Carefully, he unloaded the gun, dropped the bullet back in the battery box, and returned the gun to its hiding place among the box springs of Brent's bed. He cried because on this particular beer-soaked night, with his son still dead and his wife still alive, he had to be the luckiest son of a bitch in Alabama.

4

Deborah

The summer wagged on, punctuated by powerful afternoon thunderstorms that whipped the rotting swing against the trunk of Nonny's oak. Three times Deborah and Nonny huddled for what protection the utility room could afford.

"Shh, gal," Nonny said as she barred the door by throwing a two by four onto the ready brackets. "The storm will pass over us if we're dead quiet." So they sat on the floor of the tiny room, the only light sifting in mottled shafts through the spaces where the door didn't quite fit in its frame. Deborah figured if the storm could hear them, then it could surely see them, too, and this must be why Nonny insisted on riding out the storm in the dark.

As Deborah's eyes adjusted to the gloom, she began to notice safety issues that must have escaped Nonny's eye. The utility room was more a pantry than anything else, although Nonny's washing machine did have its place in the far corner. The rest of the tiny room was lined floor to ceiling with shelves of Mason jars, many of which held spiders rather than food. A solitary bulb was suspended from the ceiling on a wire. From its pull dangled the single item in the room, or in the house for that matter, that might be considered ostentatious: an intricately carved wooden ship. The ship was small enough to hold in the palm of Deborah's hand. It had a natural patina and was clearly very old. The ship was suspended by its mainmast, the knot secured up under the tiny crow's nest, connected to an electric sun while it sailed endlessly on invisible eddies of air.

Flashes of lightning illuminated the ship in stop-action bursts as Deborah sat in obedient silence with the tempest just over the rooftop. The mason jars shuddered with the percussive impact of the next boom of thunder, clinking in fear or protest of the noise. The suspended ship tacked and began a slow arc. Deborah strained to see in the punch-drunk brilliance that was gone almost before her eyes could register it. Nonny was stock-still, maybe even asleep in their barricaded cocoon against the storm, but Deborah was restless, eager for the noisy battering on the tin roof above to come to a stop so she could leave the catacomb din of the enclosed utility room.

Back before everything happened, she found a book in the school library about the underworld beneath Paris, France. It was an odd book tucked in beside the popular *13 Alabama Ghosts and Jeffery*. Lots of kids loved stories about spirits and haints, especially true stories. Deborah was no different in that regard and even had a pilfered copy of the Alabama book squirreled away at home. It was overdue by three school years. The French book was more like an encyclopedia than a collection of ghost stories, but it was filled with spooky black and white photos of stacks and stacks of dead folks holding up the streets of Paris with their bones. It was easy to imagine the utility room as a chamber deep within those ancient catacombs.

Claustrophobic, her breath became as ragged as Nonny's was even. Nonny's breath stank of fried onions and old woman, a contagion that only exacerbated the dank odor of the rows and rows of jars holding vegetables and meats preserved well before her birth. They were embalmed with cobwebbery and the unmistakably astringent odor of bleach. Everything in the room reeked of age and creeping rot, everything except Deborah. It filled her nostrils and her mind. As the storm pelted the roof with daggered raindrops, she let herself remember. She slid past Brent's gruesome accident, Fat Sarah's crazed death in another storm, Grandpa's slip, and into recollections that weren't altogether her own. The transition was so seamless, she felt no delineation between imagination and memory, only an overwhelming sense of disillusionment that she mistook for disapproval from her absent mother.

The ship sailed onward on its tether; traveling in a relentless sea of inky darkness without getting anywhere at all. Deborah knew just how the imaginary passengers of that ship felt. Sometimes, the journey was fascinating: at other times, frightening. Sometimes, they felt free, a salt-sprayed breeze urging them forward to better days. Happiness was possible, and she could see the future like a beacon scouring the darkness specifically to illuminate her to safety—she, herself… a fearfully and wonderfully made treasure more valuable than rubies. She imagined a younger, no older, no… historical version of herself, gossamer hair not shorn but flowing like spun gold behind her as she rode the swells. Her eyes brimmed with a hope her current persona forfeited, buried with her brother in a grave tamped down with her mother's silent condemnation and her grandmother's grim-lipped disapproval.

Deborah's sense of connection with this seafaring version of herself was so strong, she found herself peering up through the darkness to check for any evidence of loneliness in the girl's face. Because she naturally projected her own emotion onto the girl of her reverie, there had to be some undercurrent of sorrow or, more accurately, of guilt. They were alike that way; they had to be. A flash of lightning illuminated the hanging boat once again. In that instant of light, Deborah saw a metallic reflection in the hull. It was a hinge; a miniscule hinge! Deborah understood that she and this ship were one, moored and holding closely guarded secrets.

The pounding on the metal roof dwindled to a staccato pattering. Thunder rolled in the distance, searching out some other victim or poor soul without the good sense to conceal herself during the worst of it.

"Pull that light cord, Little Debbie. The storm's passed us by," ordered Nonny equably. She worked her way up from her seat on the concrete floor, using the barricade as a handhold

26

before lifting it off its cradle and propping it between the washing machine and the wall.

Deborah tried to sound nonchalant. "Nonny, is there a story behind this boat lamp puller?" She hoped it wouldn't be a long, lecture-style story.

"Of course there is. It was a little whatnot given to me… oh, I suwanee, I can't rightly recall if it was my grandmother or her grandmother. I forget the particulars. It was a favorite trinket. Probably, some fellow who didn't have the misfortune to be one of your grandpas passed it along as a token of his love. Anyhow, my mama had it on the shelf where she hung her washboard. She never would let me play with it. Ha! I recall she tore up my rear end with a switch when she caught me a-sailin' it in the washtub. It disappeared after that because she hid it in a copper spittoon way up on a shelf. I found it when I was clearing out her things after she met the Lord. It must've meant a good deal to her, to want to hide it and not let me touch it, but I never learnt why, so I kept hold of it. You know I'm not one for doo-dads, so I put it to work keeping the light here in the utility room. I figure it was a fitting place since my mama spent most of her life either washin' or puttin' up vegetables. Now, why do you ask?"

"Oh, no reason really, Nonny. I was just sort of studying on it while the cloud blew over." Deborah didn't make a peep about the hinge she'd seen. Maybe the doo-dad had kept its secret from Nonny.

"Well, let's get out of this crypt and set down to a bite of lunch," Nonny said as she opened the door and ushered Deborah toward the kitchen.

"Nonny, will you show me how to do the washing? I'd like to do a little more while I'm here with you taking care of me." Deborah needed some excuse to get back into the utility room without Nonny's prying.

"Well, well. Looks like The Good Book's finally got a foothold on your damned little soul. It says, 'Cleanliness is next to Godliness,' you know. I'll teach you after lunch, and then you

27

can do our washing from now on. I may be able to get you through them Pearly Gates despite what your mama thinks." Nonny said all of this with such uncommon brightness that the last jab hardly stung at all.

"May I bring in a little chair so I can do my reading while the clothes wash?" Deborah simpered sweetly. She could sense victory.

"Doing the Lord's work and reading the Lord's Word? I think that's a fine idea. Now, let's get to makin' that lunch."

Deborah followed Nonny into the kitchen, a picture of obedience. Her smile was true. She had won, and it was surprisingly easy.

5

Deborah

In the height of Alabama summer, the air is thick with humidity. On the worst days, it rises in waves but has nowhere to go. The heat covers the fields, the houses, the swamps, and even the mountainsides with a caul. Cats doze in the branches of trees, hoping for the air to move, which it does in slow, indolent vortices that offer little comfort. Cows stand in ponds warm as bath water, swatting at vermin with a detached boredom and the bovine wisdom of resignation. Dogs lie up under porches or dig wallows in the dirt to keep the gnats off of them. The gnats hover lazily in clouds as they live out their short lives riding on the misery of whatever monstrous creature, man or beast, who must endure the sweltering heat.

The respite carried on the heels of the storms is short-lived. Hot breezes precede thunderheads that build into towers, rage, and spend themselves all in a matter of minutes. Sometimes the rain doesn't fall, and others, it falls in sheets. For a few blessed moments beyond the rain, the press of the humidity is lifted, and a person can breathe easily, can feel cleansed, can move beyond the drugged malaise of deep summer. But summer is loath to release its grip and quickly regroups, gathering its heat from the ground up like an overprotective mother wrapping her child in layer upon layer of swaddling until the poor babe whimpers helplessly in the excess of her binding love.

The stolen moments in the utility room became Deborah's respite from Nonny's rules and routines. They marked her week with a washing-powder freshness even amidst the viscid canning jars. She found a furtive freedom smack in the middle of Nonny's Bible-hard discipline, and she guarded this newfound privacy closely by painting a thick coat of duty, appreciation, and thankfulness over her deceit. It felt good.

Deborah was careful. Nonny broached no lollygagging and often told her, "Girls who could be trusted with little would soon be trusted with much." She figured Nonny just meant she would be given more chores to do once she finally met Nonny's exacting standards, so Deborah wasn't too keen on doing a bang-up job on any given task except for the wash.

If she wanted her chance to discover what was inside that old ship, she had to know her way around the utility room. The first couple of times, she did the wash under Nonny's close supervision. There was no time to get her hands on the ship what with the precise measuring of washing powder, bleach, and borax going on. Nonny was quite concerned about the tub losing its balance. If it did, the machine would commence hopping, barge into the shelf, and shake the canning jars of prehistoric vegetables right off onto the concrete floor where they'd shatter into a mess of broken glass and curdled squash.

"I don't know what you'd die of first, Little Debbie," Nonny giggled, "lockjaw from the rusty lids, gangrene from slicing your feet up, or botulism from the pickles." Deborah recognized precisely where Mom got her proclivity for gloom and doom scenarios.

"Why don't you just throw out those old jars, Nonny?" asked Deborah.

"They, Lawd, child! Hands worked mighty hard to put up food for hard times. We can't let it go to waste."

"But, Nonny, it's too old to eat!"

"You'd be surprised what folks can eat if times get hard enough. No, Little Debbie, we'll just leave them jars be. They ain't doin' no harm 'less you get careless. They'll be jus' fine so long as you don't let that a-wash-tub lose its balance," Nonny said and fixed Deborah with a stare that left little doubt as to who'd take the blame if any of the old canning jars got broken.

The utility room was hardly bigger than a closet. Aside from the wall that held the washing machine—there was no dryer like Mom had back on July Mountain—the room was surrounded in floor to ceiling shelves, obviously homemade and markedly well-constructed, the handiwork of her long-dead grandfather. The space above the washing machine was also jar-lined shelving, with the lowest shelf cleared for washing powders, bleach, stain-fighters, and the like. The washing machine jutted out into the room and the reading chair Deborah hauled in, a rusted metal folding chair just like the ones in the Sunday School room up at the church, pretty much took up the remaining floor space. A naked light bulb was fixed in the exact center of the room, the wooden ship suspended on a chain a few inches above Deborah's head. It was largely ignored by Nonny, just a part of the landscape of the utility room now that a switch plate had been installed outside the doorway. Deborah reckoned it must've been too much of a chore for Nonny to reach up and pull the cord when she had a basket full of clothes. There were no windows so that the utility room could double as a storm shelter. The two by four that barred the door reinforced the weak spot Nonny feared a bad storm might find.

On the shelf nearest the door, another space had been cleared of canning jars, and a gallon pitcher of water had its place. Deborah was made to use that pitcher to water Nonny's houseplants, which were all of the same variety and decorated every flat surface in the living room in a sort of funereal display that unnerved Deborah but seemed to give Nonny solace—from what, Deborah wasn't sure, but she figured Nonny might have an inkling of her madness, what with talking to her dead husband and all every week. The vegetation was lush and variegated and Nonny would stroke the snaky fronds as she passed through the hub of her small house, sometimes humming what sounded like a melancholy lullaby.

31

Finally, curiosity coupled with the abject isolation of her exile from July Mountain compelled Deborah to ask Nonny about the plants. "Why do you only keep one kind of plant? What are they? Do they ever make flowers?" She fired off the questions rapidly and a bit over-eagerly before realizing she'd get a lecture, but not really minding because she needed to hear something aside from the voices in her own head. Even a cold word is better than no word at all. Unless she was being preached to or preached at, Nonny was not one for idle conversation. Nonny's gruffness was like those plants, stiff and spiky, but the thorns on the ends don't stick. Still, Deborah didn't want to cross Nonny. Mom and Daddy would never take her back if Nonny couldn't straighten her out, whatever that meant.

"Some folks call these snake plants; some call them Saint George's sword. Most folks around here call them mother-in-law's tongue," Nonny began. "My grandmother believed they warded off bad spirits and always kept a pot by her front door. She probably got that notion from old darky stories because the Bible has nothing to say on the matter. I believe the encyclopedia says the plants came out of Africa. You know the Bible scholars say that the Garden of Eden was somewhere in Africa. Maybe these were the plants that guarded its gates when the Lord evicted Old Adam and Eve."

Nonny was on a roll now, and Deborah was listening closely because she recognized a pattern. "Now, you know we don't hold them Papists any count, and we sure don't go around praying to no saints of the olden days. That's not what the Good Book teaches. Old Saint George, though, was the one who killed a dragon. Lookee here. These fronds are as long as a sword and just as stiff to the touch. They're poisonous, too. They bleed or sweat just like we do, but one drop on the tongue will give you the runs for a week. Won't kill you, but they'll make you wish you were dead. Come to think of it, that might be the very reason why some folks call them mother-in-law's tongue," Nonny chortled at her joke but then shifted into a deeper, murkier tone.

32

"I see your mind a-turnin' just as plain as if you were speaking out loud, Little Debbie. You're thinking about how these plants are like those dolls your mama keeps a-hangin' on your bedroom wall. Maybe so. But ponder this whilst you're studying on whether I'm the one who's crazy: walls can be made of all sorts of things, plants or even dolls. What you really need to know is whether those walls are protecting what's inside 'em or what's outside 'em. Now, the real question is... she paused for effect... on which side of the wall are you standing?" As odd as it seemed, this was the most prescient lecture Nonny had delivered since Deborah loaded up her suitcase after the funeral. Surprisingly, Nonny had even more to say.

"Gal, your mama ain't done right by you, and that's a shame. You're lucky to be staying a spell with your grandmother so I can show you how things are. Your mama denying the truth and trying to stomp down your sight is what's got your brother kilt if you ask me. That's why she don't know what to do with 'ya. I didn't know what to do with her, either, so I guess we're all in the same boat. Ain't nothin' but hardship for us Clemm women no-how."

"What do you mean, Nonny?"

"You know as well as I do that ghosts is real. You see me doin' what I can to keep your granddaddy in the ground where he belongs. Anyone who tries to tell you ghosts ain't real is just blind. Hell, ghosts is even in the Bible, for Christ sake."

"But, Nonny, she's not just a ghost, is she?" It was the first time Deborah even mentioned what Mom called her grandmother ageless. Surprised as she was that Mom shared her secret, she was even more surprised to learn it was no secret to Nonny. What if they all quit keeping secrets? This wasn't a happy secret, though, and Deborah, like her mother and grandmother, felt the need to swallow it up rather than get it out and turn it about in the light. It brought up too many questions that she didn't really want the answer to. Maybe that's what secrets are all about, not the silly ones like who ate the last of the cookies, but the deep ones,

33

the ones families pass down and hide for generations. They were invisible walls built around a person's good name. Maybe they protected the person within. Maybe they protected the persons without. Either way, it wasn't a good idea to go chipping away at the wall. Who knows what lies on the other side?

This made Deborah think of the kids at school laughing at her when she reasoned that Santa Claus must be real because why would there be so many stories, TV shows, and even news reports if he were a phony? Even when she realized the presents came from Mom and Daddy, a deeper doubt niggled at her. If all the grown-ups kept the real identity of Santa a secret, working together to perpetuate his story, couldn't the same be true about God? These were questions she couldn't ask her parents without revealing her disbelief. Mom reminded her and Brent that children without faith in Santa didn't get any presents on Christmas morning. Her curiosity wasn't as strong as her greed. She didn't want to be left out. If faith worked the same with God, she would be deeply disappointed. This was one of the answers she sought as she was reading the Bible this interminable summer. So far, it was silent on both Santa Claus and how to get hold of that faith people who get to see God are supposed to have.

Nonny took Deborah by the shoulders, squared them toward her, and brought herself down to eye level. Her voice was low and scary, bringing Deborah out of her tangled-up thoughts. She spoke slowly and deliberately. "You let this burn in, child: She's in our blood—yours, your mother's, mine—there's no escapin' that."

"I don't understand," Deborah whined. "Why does she haunt us?"

"Whyever not? She's part of who we are. She appears at her whim, and she always brings despair. That's why we don't go invitin' her. That's why your mama tried to shield you from her. Now, she finally understands we can't stop her from settin' her evil in motion." Nonny's voice was barely above a whisper, as if she feared the haint might overhear.

34

"So, we're cursed?"

Nonny laughed in an explosive cackle and then leaned in extra close. "Cursed? I wish it were that simple. No, Little Debbie, we're not cursed. We're damned, the whole lot of us."

6

Nonny

It took a few weeks to get Nonny settled into the routine of the newer, better, laundry-responsible Deborah. She knew she had Nonny convinced when Nonny hollered from the living room, "Pull that door to! I can't hear my story over the spin cycle!"

Deborah hated "Story Time" even if it was the only program Nonny watched on TV, aside from The *Price Is Right* and the local news. That mean babysitter who gave her nothing but cheese sandwiches and nasty chocolate bars while she helped herself to the family's food watched soap operas all day long. Deborah couldn't remember much about her besides her enormity and an even bigger cruelty. The woman's name and face were lost to the past. After all, it had been years since the tree landed on the cow, years where Mom and Daddy never mentioned her, never talked about the terrible storm that almost took her and her brother.

"What's past is past," Daddy said, "It won't do nobody a damn lick of good to go dwellin' there." So, that part of the past just sort of faded, erased by time and silence, a powerful tonic for a growing girl.

Her aversion to chocolate remained, though. Deborah couldn't abide the stuff. It was like choking down medicine or guilty promises. She flat out refused chocolate candy bars, but nibbled miserably out of nervous politeness on the chocolaty confections Nonny made when she first came to live in the lonely brick house. Cake, brownies, and even Nonny's "famous" chocolate pie recipe that captured her grand-daddy's heart would go largely untouched. Nonny finally declared, "Well, I suwanee. What an odd child it is who won't eat chocolate!"

Now, Nonny only made chocolate flavored treats when Deborah displeased her, which was still fairly frequently. Nonny's displeasure was expressed in *tsking* tongue clicks, pointed looks, "I suwanees," and the appearance of chocolate. Aside from the chocolate, this pretty much constituted Nonny's natural disposition, so Deborah spent most of the summer trying to figure out when Nonny was disappointed in the world in general or her in particular. It was an odd dance; a girl on the cusp of adolescence looking ahead to what must become better times and a grandmother on the brink of the grave looking back on the time she had and finding it lacking.

Nonny could have imparted wisdom. She could have embraced her granddaughter and faced the morass of the damnable blood legacy they shared, even shouldered some of the burden, but she was worn out. She tried once before, long ago, with Caroline. Tried and failed. The only way to survive, no endure, for ultimately, survival was out of the question, was to harden her heart and to harden the girl's.

Caro needed time to lick her wounds, to soothe the pain of losing her son at the hands of the haint. Nonny didn't believe for a second that Brent's death was accidental as the deputy's report stated. Too much sad coincidence surrounded Little Debbie—too much death too soon. She knew it when the child emerged unscathed from that killer storm. Caro knew it, too, though she refused to admit it. Now, Caro had a true, undeniable taste of the despair parceled out for her.

She'd never get over the loss of her son. It was an exquisite torture that would lurk in the shadows of her mind for all her days. Some days and many nights, her failure as a mother would come to the forefront, a stabbing pain as real as Saint Paul's fleshy thorn. These were the times that would be as unbearable as the sharp labor pains that brought her boy into the world. She

37

would bear it, though, because there was nothing to do but bear it. What Nonny knew, what Caro was learning, and what Little Debbie had yet to experience was that despite what balm the word of the Lord offered, there was no deliverance from the sharp agony of a dead child.

Little Debbie's connection with her grandmother ageless—as Caro so prettily candy-coated that damned mean-spirited she-devil—was solid. In her most honest recollections, it was evident from the moment the mewling little thing peered up from her bassinet and fixed her with a gaze whose intensity spoke of centuries of knowledge. Nonny half expected the babe to speak full-blown sentences. The silent exchange marked a moment of clarity: this girl was claimed. She dared not love the child, nor in due time the grandson who followed. She dared not play the doting grandmother for fear the haint would strike out of spite. Her own grandmother tried to warn her, to make her understand the tendency of blood tempered with too much sweetness to curdle. Her own grandmother spoke of a gathering misery that would strike each daughter in due time, but in her own youthful optimism, buoyed up by love or more accurately, lust, she discounted her grandmother's prediction as the ramblings of a bitter, old woman

Now, she played the role of the bitter, old woman. Her heart, shriveled as the skin on her hands that no amount of lotion could smooth, still beat, though. It was relentless in its pounding. It was unlimited in the amount of pain it could swallow. It took in the ones she loved, chewing up her soul, as it beat onward. The real curse, far more terrible than the whorish vengeance of a common haint, was the curse of endurance.

The Family Bible, a largely unread coffee table copy kept for company to witness as proof of salvation, told the story in its front pages titled "Family Record." This Bible sat in its esteemed place in her house, her mother's house, and as she recalled, her grandmother's house before that. It was passed down to the matriarch of each generation who was charged with recording the dates of births, marriages, and deaths of the family in her neatest hand. It was an heirloom not to be touched by children or profaned by the sinful eyes of readers. Its pages still crackled despite its age when she shakily set in ink her grandson's demise just a few months ago.

Brent Isom Ballard, 1972-1982, broken neck: go-cart accident.

She hadn't opened it since; even said a prayer to be granted the mercy of never having to open it again. She had endured enough. God-willing, the next entry would be in Caro's hand.

She rested in patterns, a labyrinthine ritual of behaviors she believed kept the haint and the despair she brought with her at bay. If she remained where she should be when she should be there, their paths would only intersect the final time. This is where she placed her faith much more so than in the walls of that little church across the road from the cemetery.

But when she took Little Debbie in, the greatest act of love she had mustered in decades, she invited death as well. The child stank of it, an earthy rot just this side of perception. It permeated her pores. When she laundered the girl's bedclothes, she picked up the faintest scent of burned flesh and smiled at the haint's cruelty. No amount of bleach could completely mask it. Nonny rationalized her old memory was just playing tricks on her and the smell wasn't penance for the greed that baked her boy in that truck all those years ago.

Rationalization is always a choice bandage for truth. It only covers the wound for a while, but eventually the truth seeps through with its undeniable pus. The Bible talks about reckoning and the Great Judgment when every person will be called to account for his or her shortcomings. "I know a thing or two about reckoning," Nonny muttered to herself, "and I damn sure know about being washed in blood."

39

Women have armored themselves in patterns for ages. Even the nursery rhymes speak of it. Simple children's verses pass down not only what to do but when to do it. Nonny kept to the old ways for the most part, modern convenience only altering tradition slightly. Firmly believing upsetting the pattern could spell disaster, Nonny took refuge in the pattern itself—washing Monday, ironing Tuesday, mending Wednesday, weeding Thursday, cleaning Friday, baking Saturday, and resting Sunday—spinning round and round the mulberry bush world without end.

The old dances moved in patterns, too, braiding a thick plait of friendship as girls learned the steps together and later whirled their way into the heart of a beau. The names change over the years—minuet, waltz, reel—but their magic twines tightly into the fabric of expectation, warping and weaving a cloak of security for those who move within its folds. Nonny felt almost sorry for Little Debbie who would come of age in a time when the dance has lost its soul, denigrated to abandoned gyrations and the monotonous driving beats of music that is as far too simple as it is too loud.

Even when the young people slow down, they do little more than a shuffling grope. Why, it is practically public masturbation. Nonny blushed at that sudden unbidden revelation and shrugged her shoulders at what the world was coming to these days. It was all going to Hell in a hand-basket. She wouldn't live long enough to see the chaos that would ensue in the Final Days and was thankful for that mercy. Little Debbie might get to see the end, though. It would be an unsought for, unwelcome, but necessary gift... like giving a child socks and underwear for her birthday. Nonny couldn't see Kingdom Come as victorious glory; it would be a bittersweet farewell.

Hell, come to think of it, she even slept under patterns. Her great-grandmother's hand-stitched quilts, dry-rotted in places, still blanketed the beds of her house. Perhaps they would cover her own great-grandchildren, lulling them with the comfort and serenity of a past they would mistake for simpler times. Her favorite was deceptive in its plainness. The quilt depicted interlocking circles in faded pastels of various fabrics resting on a field of white, which was now unevenly yellowed with age and the countless pissings of little ones. The quilting itself was stitched in fist-sized hearts instead of the sewn squares that held the batting inside the rest of the family quilts in her collection. These hearts covered the entire area of the quilt, the cleft of their humps forming the point of another heart..., a sea of hearts stitched in the same color as whatever part of the design they covered, smothering whoever would lie beneath in an almost transparent blanket of love.

The interlocking circles, like wedding bands, suggested infinity and fertility in a simultaneous gasp. It was a family story—as old quilts tend to be—but one based in heartbreak that would eventually evolve into a kind of hope, or at the least, a source of warmth. Nonny took this quilt as a wedding gift from her mother who was given the quilt as a wedding gift by her mother before her, and so on. Nobody really knew how far back. It had undergone repairs and additions over the years, each mother putting her hand to the quilt. Large enough to touch the floor on either side of the bed and overlaid in spots, the quilt was a testament to the handicraft lost to industrialization.

The quilt captured the imaginations of children with its varied scraps of fabric, some dainty and some rugged, some soft in color and some spots boldly patterned. Parts of the quilt were worn threadbare with age while other parts had not been ravaged by time. The oldest daughters knew the quilt would grace their wedding beds; it was a longstanding family tradition. They traced their fingers around the inlaid hearts, feeling for hints at the frightening unknown bliss awaiting them.

Nonny's mother kept the secret of the quilt until it was time to jar Nonny back into living, just months after sweet little Bedford was laid to rest. Nonny, distraught, had taken to her own bed unable to face the monotony of a forever without her son.

Levin begged her to come out of the room and care for Caro, care for him, but she spewed venom at them both, blaming them for Bedford's death.

"If you hadn't waited to sell that cotton, we'd still have our son. *You* killed him, you greedy son of a bitch! Why did he lock the doors? Why didn't you bust out the windows? Why didn't you die rather than leave your son to the flames?" she shouted. He blanched and shut the door behind him. When Caro, dressed in her Sunday best braids and ribbons tried to rouse her for church, she unleashed her vehemence on her daughter, telling her she wished it were Caro who died in the conflagration rather than Bedford. Shortly thereafter, Levin fetched Nonny's mother to talk some sense into her daughter and do for the living members of the family until his wife could get a handle on her grief.

Already brittle-boned, Nonny's mother barely weighted the mattress as she sat down silently and ran her hand gently over the quilt. She started muttering names, at first low and then in a kind of sing-song dirge, a lullaby in minor. "Benjamin, Asher, Myrtle, Joe," she crooned, "so many others I don't know." Her arthritic finger followed the interlocking hearts. "Your turn has come to stitch your sorrow into this quilt, Noneen Clematis. It will tuck you in, keep you warm, and you shall never forget your boy. This is how we go on. This is how we survive when our hearts have been rent in two. Place your hand on this mourning quilt, Noneen. Keep its beautiful secret until the time is right for your daughter or granddaughter someday. The tears of your mothers are held inside, batted by the memories of the babes they lost. You can keep your Bedford right here."

"I always thought it was called a morning quilt because the colors are lovely like the morning light," Nonny replied. Somehow it was comforting to know her grandmothers suffered grief this wrenching. It made her feel less alone, less vulnerable to the caprices of fate.

"This quilt comforts those who are mourning and those yet to mourn. Even when it wears to thread, its remnants will caress

42

your aching heart. It's our gift from mother to mother to be," Nonny's mother added with a nod.

After a few more days of sobbing, Nonny got out of bed, gathered her sewing materials, and appliqued the front pocket from the bib of Bedford's smart red overalls onto the mourning quilt. She planned its position carefully, not really minding that her child's memory overshadowed that of another lost to time. As she finally slept in those early days, and as was her current habit all these decades later, her arm rested on top of the quilt with her hand tucked inside the red denim pocket of her little boy.

Nonny admired the mourning quilt draped on her bed, its one pocket now faded from the wear of her fingers clenching and grasping in the night. Nonny was a fair to middling quilter herself, but she used a sewing machine and printed fabrics bought specifically for that purpose. She followed a pattern suggested by the manufacturer. When it occurred to her there were tens of thousands of old women working through their change of years on identical quilting kits out of a mail-order catalog, the blessed monotony of the craft lost its luster, and she dismantled the quilting frame.

She decided the best she could do was to preserve the quilts stitched out of practicality and perhaps even love by her mothers. She kept them folded and protected in trash bags for years, not really knowing what to do with the old things, but having enough sense not to throw them away. The only one she actually slept under was the mourning quilt.

After Levin busted his brains out, she rediscovered the rest of the old quilts shoved in the back of a closet as she was clearing out his earthly remains. She chuckled out loud, even after all these years, thinking of her one act of vengeance against a marriage that was dead long before he was. She sacked up his clothes and shoes, even his undershirts and shorts, wrapped up and folded neat as you please, and dropped them off at the doorstep of a government housing project office clear over in Huntsville. It'd sure enough goad him to think a colored man might be wearing his drawers and walking in his shoes, and that tickled her. Served him right.

Nonny thought about her mother's rare act of kindness, the gentleness with which she revealed the true purpose of the mourning quilt all those years ago when grief had her in its clutches and how that revelation gave her a toehold to pull herself out of the depths of despair. It made her look less harshly at their fractured relationship and her own failure to make amends with Caro.

7

Deborah

Deborah stood silently in the chair, examining the ship's sleek hull. The washing machine's spin cycle would mask any noise if she were careless, but she wouldn't be careless. She pulled a tiny screwdriver, pilfered from Nonny's glasses kit, from the waistband of her terrycloth shorts. She hoped it would be just the thing to pry open the hinge. The boost from the chair gave Deborah an excellent vantage point. She held the ship steady in her right hand and experimented gingerly with the screwdriver, poking and gently scraping at the rust on the hinge. She had to figure out how to open it without breaking it.

She was tired of illusions and harboring secrets that were known but rarely, if ever, spoken of. This, she was certain, was a true secret... something she could hold onto for herself, treasure up in her heart, and keep. The tragedy of the spring and the loneliness of the summer taught her that the things she thought made her unlike anyone else she knew weren't unique. She couldn't decide what she resented more..., the fact she shared this ghostly secret with her mother and grandmother, or the fact that they actively tried to keep the secret from her grasp.

What if her true abilities were retarded by all the denial and secrecy? What if those vague memories of that giant tree, the recurring dreams, and the occasional presence of her grandmother ageless held more meaning than Nonny and Mom let on? Deborah knew she was bright, even wily in her ability to read the truth beneath people's words and discover their secrets. So, why had she not been able to read the secrets her mother and grandmother kept sealed in silence? What had they sacrificed to keep them from her?

The answer somehow was held inside this ancient ship in her hand. Deborah stretched on her toes, slippery with sweat, but grasping hard on the edge of the chair as it wobbled with her effort. She brought her nose up to the ship and breathed in the deep earthy smell of wood worn slick with the caresses of many years.

She ran her thumb along the underbelly and felt the wood give beneath it. The hinge was not like a door hinge; it was a slide mechanism! Her scrapings had loosed it enough to be pliable. If luck was on her side, she'd be able to slide the trapdoor open, take out the contents, and return it to its original state without Nonny being the wiser. She shook the ship gently to determine if something was moving around in its cavity, but she couldn't detect any movement. Deborah glanced at her wristwatch; she had three minutes left in the spin cycle.

She opened her mouth in concentration and applied pressure to the sealed door. An old storybook image of God's hand closing the door to Noah's ark while the rain poured down on the unlucky people and animals of the world came to mind as it began to slide open on what felt like a gritty track. Her mind racing with possibilities, Deborah took a jagged breath. She stretched upward just a hair more and felt her toes slide on the chair below. She willed herself not to fall as the miniature door moved, showering her open palm and upturned face with a fine dust that tasted of bark and age. Deborah sputtered to get the substance out of her mouth. She tipped the boat, stern down, then quickly upended it. Into her hand fell a mostly decomposed acorn and a pebble. She moved her thumb back to reposition the trap door, hopped silently from the chair, and slipped her treasures into the waistband of her joggers all as the washing machine announced its completed task with a discordant buzzer.

Deborah ran her hand through her choppy hair to dislodge any dust that may have settled there and used her feet to kick

46

what was left toward the corners of the utility room. She was careful not to disturb any of the shelves and tinkle the glass jars. She did not want to alert Nonny to anything being amiss. She swept the seat of the chair with her hand to clean off any footprints and picked the Bible up from where she had left it on the floor—a whipping offense on its own—to place it on the chair before gathering up the clothes in their rattan basket. Nonny insisted that the clothes be taken out of the washing machine immediately after spinning so that they wouldn't "spoil" in the washer. The treasures cut into her bare skin as she lugged the basket out to the clothesline. That's how she assured herself of their safety. She hastily hung the clothes up to bake-dry in the heat, being certain to hide the unmentionables behind the polyester pantsuits and t-shirts so that the company who might come a-calling, but never did, wouldn't be shocked that Nonny owned underwear and knee-highs.

All the while, the contents of the drifting ship dug at her waist while the sense of it all dug at her mind. She didn't know what she would find, but the reader in her expected something more exciting than an acorn and a rock. She had hoped she would find a connection to her past, maybe even to Renae Clemence, although she had no desire ever to meet the haint face to face again. At least she no longer had to doubt the reality of her ghostly ancestor. Her mother and grandmother both believed she was real. She was slowly learning who she was and what she is, but she had no idea of the why's, and she had no idea how she fit into the puzzle.

Deborah found herself in the old swing looking up at the branches of the worn oak. Nonny would be caught up in the goings on of her soap opera for close to fifteen more minutes, so she reached into her waistband to pull out the acorn and pebble. She felt let down, as she did every Christmas after the gifts had been opened and she'd catalogued her haul. That sense of it being over was a disappointment hard to shake. For Deborah, most of the fun of Christmas was found in the anticipation, the waiting.

She enjoyed the preparation much more than the feast itself. Once it was over, she wanted it to be over. She couldn't understand why anyone would want to linger over the season. What's done is done.

She couldn't shake that feeling, what Mom labeled her After-Christmas Blues, even though she sat in the sweltering afternoon heat of summer with only the fake breeze of the rickety swing offering solace in its motion. She fingered the acorn and brought it up to her nose. It smelled like any other rotting acorn, nothing special. It must have meant something to her ancestor at some point, but now it was worthless trash. She tossed it on the ground beneath the swing, one acorn in a sea of acorns in various stages of rot.

It was hard to believe that a tree of the stature of the one towering above her could emerge from a single acorn. It took decades for an oak to reach maturity and even more decades for it to decay from the inside out. All of this, of course, was dependent on a good deal of luck in the face of the inevitable. The tree had to withstand storms and progress. Builders took down huge trees every day to clear space for shopping malls. Farmers cut them down for firewood and burned the stumps to clear their fields of obstacles. Families picnicked in their shade and buried their dead dogs amongst the roots. Girls dreamed under their canopies, and lovers snuck kisses behind their trunks.

What had this tree seen? Who planted its acorn, or had it just sprung up from the loamy earth unbidden by man? That idea titillated Deborah in that a tree observes both good and evil, and stands for them both. Maybe one of her grandmothers saw trees the same way. Maybe the girl who owned the toy boat kept the acorn because she loved trees as Deborah did. Maybe this tree was old enough to love them both.

Deborah peered up through the branches as she reclined on the swing and began to rub the dusty pebble on her shorts leg so that she could get a better look at it. The light dappled beneath the leaves, casting moving shadows as the upper branches trembled on eddies she was unable to feel below. She turned the pebble over in her palm. At first, she thrilled to the thought that it wasn't a pebble but a priceless pearl. Closer inspection revealed a more revolting truth: it was a tooth, a worthless tooth. Still, why would this be a keepsake? Deborah could not believe that the ship was simply a Tooth Fairy receptacle because the ship itself was too exquisitely made.

Also, it had been kept for so many years by her grandmother and great-grandmother before that. There had to be more to the story, even if it was just a lamp pull now. If Nonny's mother and grandmothers were as secretive as her own mom had been, she may never know the story. The story might not matter a whit, or it could mean everything. Deborah sighed, tucked the tooth back in her waistband, and walked back to the house thoroughly disappointed.

***

Just like that the waking dreams returned. Deborah didn't need to stretch beyond the mountain of pillows to find the clock with her eyes, but she couldn't stand the uncertainty of it. Somehow, if the digital readout broadcast one a.m. or even three a.m. things would be all right. She waited, willing herself back to a sleep she knew would not come until she paid the price. She drifted awhile in that state of semi-consciousness between waking and sleeping, that state where she might startle herself with the involuntary jumping of a limb. It was a feeling that unnerved her because it caused her to imagine someone or something had pressed its weight on her bed, her leg recoiling in reflex of the repulsive thing that joined her.

Still, Deborah refused to open her eyes…, refused to turn to the clock…, and slid her foot carefully under the safety of the comforter. Although her eyes were exposed to the night, the rest of her was tucked away, clean up to her nose. She took a careful breath, expecting that familiar off-putting odor, and there it was.

49

It was an earthy smell, just this side of rot. Her mouth tasted of dust, and she thought of the tethered ship hanging in the utility room. It was making circles, sailing frantically through the inky darkness, orbit widening on an invisible current.

Stiff with fright, Deborah lay stark still, trying not to breathe the contagion that stagnated the air around her. Reason staked a claim in her mind—the fetid odor was her own night breath settling in the covers around her mouth; it was just her own rancid fart rousing her from her sleep, but reason couldn't explain the presence. Reason couldn't explain the surety that, if she opened her eyes, she would be staring into the face of death itself.

It was breathing onto her, into her, and she was held in its thrall. The ship was in full arc now, its prow skating across the canning jars, and humming like a June bug tied on a string. The jars sang in response, shimmying closer to the edge of their shelf. The shelf tipped with their weight.

She was dreaming, and in her dream she had the courage to open her eyes. She saw a reflection of herself as plain as if she were looking in a mirror: shorn, tufted hair hanging about brilliant, tortured eyes that would shift color along with the sky; eyes that knew the future held no joy. This time the specter whispered her name.

"Deborah."

Her eyes popped open—no longer dreaming her wakefulness—and she sat up, the sudden motion pushing back the stale air. The clock read 3:07 a.m., and she sighed in relief. It had all been a night terror.

Across the house, glass shattered. "Renny!" escaped her lips, throaty and unbidden. Her nightgown tangled around her knees as she padded quickly to the utility room, switching on lights as she ran.

The door to the utility room was closed. Deborah took a deep breath before barging in. The bulb glared naked above her, cutting through her nightgown to silhouette puerile breasts as she slipped to her knees, hands in frenzied search through the gore of

50

congealed tomatoes. Broken shards of glass bit at her fingers as she plowed through clots of decades-old bounty. The acrid odor of rotten vegetables turned her stomach, and she retched, dry-heaving as her knees ground the crushed glass.

The mahogany ship was not there. She looked up at the frayed cord and then at the broken shelf. One end had collapsed, causing the cans of tomatoes to slide right off and burst onto the floor. Tomato juice dripped down the remaining rows of vegetables and down the washing machine. Tomato, crushed and clotted, floated in the watering bucket. Deborah crawled backward out of the room, trying not to add to the mess by vomiting. The smell was unreal. Her hands and knees were hurting, and with her nightgown dripping juice she went to the kitchen to rinse off. *Nonny's going to be mad as a hornet,* she thought before realizing Nonny's absence in all the commotion.

"Nonny!" she shouted and sprinted down the hall. She burst into Nonny's bedroom, flicked on the light, and stopped short. "Nonny?" Her grandmother lay still as death, tucked to the chin under her mourning quilt, eyes bulging as if frozen while trying to see everything at once. In her left hand, she clutched the little ship, its trap door laid bare. The room was as hot as four o'clock in August. Nonny took a ragged breath and turned her protuberant eye to Deborah.

"Renae?" she hissed. "You demon."

Nonny's lower eyelid was drooping, reaching downward to her wrinkled cheekbone. She transformed ghoulishly as she spoke, slurring more and more of her words.

"No, Nonny. It's me…, Little Debbie." Nonny ignored this, mistaking her bloodied granddaughter for the haint.

"You took our boys, Goddamn you. Goddamn you to hell where you belong! I got your damned boat; weren't nothin' but dust left of what you hid inside. I swallowed it, Goddamn you, and if I live long enough, I'll shit you out… shit you out of our lives forever or take you to hell with me," Nonny growled as a fine trickle of drool inched out of the corner of her mouth. Her

51

lower lip pulled downward. One side of her face was trying to slip off her jawbone and down onto the mourning quilt.

Terrified, Deborah staggered backward and in that shift, the stifling presence left the room with such force the door slammed.

"Missy?" Nonny gasped, recognizing her granddaughter at the foot of her bed.

"It's me, Nonny, Little Debbie…; she's gone. Renae's gone. What do I do?"

"Fetch the hammer, Deborah."

8

Deborah

The pre-dawn darkness was inky despite the westward sliver of moonlight casting the oak tree in relief. Deborah, hair standing in tufts, nightgown whipping about her bloodied knees, grasped the hammer as she sprinted barefoot through the fallow field behind her grandmother's house. Mindless of the cockle burrs snagging her gown and the stubble of volunteer weeds gouging her feet, she appeared to glide across the field. When she reached the half-rotted fence that marked the edge of the property, she flung the hammer as far as her strength would allow. Barely pausing, she turned and hoofed it back toward the oak tree, which seemed bathed in light even though she was running in darkness.

She barreled toward the trunk of the tree, sliding under the swing like a baseball player trying to score the winning run. Brent always practiced sliding like Pete Rose, belly down and fingers stretched, but she didn't like getting a face full of dirt. He called her a toe-reaching sissy, so she slid that way just to spite him, even if it did mean she'd pepper up her legs. Once she figured out to wear her sweatpants when they played ball out in the yard, she never had to worry about getting strawberries on her thighs again. Tonight, though, she had no sweatpants to protect her legs. Acorns barked against and into her leg as she cleared the swing and got up on her knees. "Get away from us! Get the hell away from us!" she seethed as she scattered the acorns out into the yard.

She needed to sweep away the bit of acorn that had fallen from the hold of the ship, sweep away whatever links to that past she could to free herself from the tyranny of blood. She refused to be a manifestation of a long-dead bitch hell-bent on stealing what little happiness she could muster. Dust and tears marked her face as she traced the moon sinking through the branches, never thinking to pray, not able to recall a single Bible verse Nonny drilled into her head to use in times of trouble.

Nonny needed help. Deborah turned toward the beauty parlor across the highway. Even though she was strictly forbidden to "get in that road," she knew the infraction would be forgiven. She looked like a specter rushing across the blacktop. Her nightgown was ripped, bloodstained, and sodden with dirt and dew. Her face, stricken with terror, looked much the same.

She beat on the door of the beauty parlor with her fists, calling out, "Mrs. Garlan! Help!" The door remained closed, and Deborah realized she probably couldn't hear her from the house, so she ran around the garage, looking for a back door. She continued screaming and scrabbling at the windows along the back of the house before coming to a glass slider. She beat on that door so viciously she thought it might shatter and rain shards on her head, but finally, she saw a light flick on in the hallway. Mrs. Garlan rounded a corner and let out such a screech when she saw Deborah, she dropped the shotgun she kept to scare off boogers.

"Mrs. Garlan! Please help us! Please help Nonny!" Deborah was so beside herself in panic she didn't even flinch at the sight of the shotgun on the floor or the tin can curlers all over Mrs. Garlan's head.

"Hush up, gal! I thought you was a ghost, you look so awful! What's happened? What have you done to your grandmother?" Mrs. Garlan fired off her questions in rapid succession as she hauled Deborah into her house and onto a couch. "Why are you filthy, girl? Is that blood? I've got plastic on that good davenport so it won't get stained, so sit down and catch your breath so you

54

can tell me what happened." Mrs. Garlan's cans rattled on her head she was so excited.

"Is the old bag dead? Did you kill her? I reckon I ought to call the sheriff. Hoo wee, you look a fright, like you've done battled your way out of a grave!" Mrs. Garlan was talking a mile a minute. One of the cans came undone and bounced off the coffee table and onto the carpet. Mrs. Garlan let out a nervous giggle and toed the can up under the couch. Deborah noticed it was a beer can, but decided just to save that up for later.

"Nobody's killed anybody, but Nonny needs help," Deborah's heart was still jumping around in her chest, and she began shivering. Mrs. Garlan picked up an afghan, then thought better of it.

"I'm gonna get a towel for you to wrap up in and some slippers for your feet. Lord knows, I might have to get the carpet shampooed after this. You just set right there a piece while I fix my hair. Then I'll drive you back over, and we'll check on your grandmamma. Don't you worry; I won't take but a minute. If I have to call the rescue squad, I can't be seen with my hair a-tizzy. It'd be bad for business. She's probably just havin' a spell. Ain't you ever seen an old woman in a spell?"

After what seemed like an eternity, but was probably only a few minutes, Mrs. Garlan reappeared pocketbook in hand and plastic headwrap in place. She had slathered on blood red lipstick and drawn some hasty eyebrow lines. She looked as ghastly as Deborah felt.

"Let's go to the car," Mrs. Garlan directed.

She moved like a frigate in those clunky heels, outpacing Deborah as she cut through a hallway and a galley kitchen whose cabinet tops were festooned in an intricate tangle of vines dripping with a bounty of waxed grapes. A large bowl of apples, also waxed, graced the countertop. Aside from that, the counters were bare, scrupulously clean, and smelling of antiseptic. Mrs. Garlan opened the door to a perfectly organized pantry and grabbed a large roll of plastic wrap before continuing to the door.

Wagging a finger at Deborah, Mrs. Garlan directed her to wait while she put a layer of cellophane on her vinyl car seat. "I don't want you mucking up my car, too. Let's go see what's ailing your grandmother, probably having to keep up with the likes of you in her old age." Mrs. Garlan used the turn-around in her driveway to get the car facing out to the road, put on her turn signal, and proceeded to pull out even though the lights of a semi were quickly growing large.

"Damn trucks. They speed through here at all hours of the night, making enough noise to raise the dead. Well, this one will just have to slow his ass down. Now don't you go reporting to whoever has ears you've heard me cussin'. I'll deny it to heaven and won't nobody believe you anyway. I'm a pillar of the Methodist Church, and you're just a scraggly-headed girl."

Almost immediately, she flipped the turn signal on in the opposite direction and brought her car to a complete stop before making the turn into Nonny's driveway. The trucker, fast approaching, screeched his brakes before thinking better of it and swung into the left lane, horn blaring as the pressure of the passing truck shook the car. Mrs. Garlan let out a laugh and gunned it into the driveway.

Deborah whipped out of the car and ran to the back door as Mrs. Garlan made her way to the front, murmuring "Don't matter that I've been doing her hair for ten years, we ain't backdoor neighbors. I'll come to the front. Ain't nobody with manners skulks around a back door." Deborah barreled down the hall and into Nonny's hot room.

"I've got help, Nonny! Here's Mrs. Garlan." Nonny was sleeping, although the lower lid of her right eye hung open and exposed the tender tissue beneath. A gnat was swarming around the eye, dipping in to drink while Nonny didn't even bother to blink. Something was terribly wrong.

Mrs. Garlan's eyes widened as she stepped into the stifling heat of Nonny's bedroom. "Why, Noneen, you've gone and had your stroke." Mrs. Garlan said this as equably as if Nonny had

56

just gone and had a slice of pecan pie, but she moved purposefully to the bedside.

"Girlie, go gather up some fresh underthings and bedclothes for your grandmamma. Sometimes ladies mess themselves when they have a stroke, and I will spare your grandmamma the indignity of having the rescue squad pull her from a puddle of piss. Thy Lord! It's hot as hell in here. Is it always this way? Scat, girl! I'll call the men. Phone in the kitchen?"

"Yes, Ma'am, right by the stove." Deborah was glad Mrs. Garlan finally sprang into action and felt the sense of relief all children feel when a capable adult, likeable or not, takes control of a sorry situation.

"Find her overnight bag," Mrs. Garlan continued as she reached the bedroom door, fanning herself with her hand. "They'll be hauling her to the hospital. Pray they don't want to take her to Huntsville. That's what they do when they think the Reaper's a pokin' around with his sickle. I sure hope he ain't skulking around here tonight."

"No, not him," Deborah muttered as Mrs. Garlan marched back up the hallway. She hightailed it to the bathroom closet where Nonny kept her sheets and towels. Instinctively, Deborah sniffed the air, testing it for that methane rot she'd recognize for the rest of her life. The only thing rotten she could detect was the stench of those ancient tomatoes wafting from her filthy nightgown.

I really need to get out of this mess, she thought, but she needed to take care of her grandmother more. Besides, she didn't want to smell the death odor—Nonny couldn't die—what would she do?

9

Garlan

Mrs. Garlan found herself in a jungle of mother-in-law's tongues she hadn't noticed when that tufty-headed girl dragged her back to Noneen's bedroom. She found her way to the kitchen, *tsked* at the rotary phone cradled on the wall, and got the rescue squad on their way. She marched back to the bedroom where the girl was waiting with some sheets.

"The rescue squad is bringing the ambulance. Let's make sure she's presentable." She stripped an old, ragged quilt, one of those hand-stitched nightmares from half a century ago, down to Noneen's ankles, looking for soiled linens. The old bag held her piss but was bare-assed under her nightgown.

"We need to get her underpants on her now. She'd never be able to face the church if everyone knew she'd been sleeping in the raw, especially being an old widow-woman."

Mrs. Garlan could barely contain the glint in her eye from this little tidbit. Of course the entire Ladies' Auxiliary would hear of this little indiscretion. Noneen groaned as they hefted her into her cotton briefs.

"It's so warm in here, she may die of heatstroke instead of just a regular stroke," Mrs. Garlan quipped, before catching the look of despair in the girl's eyes. "Oh, don't you fret. The best way to get through horrible times is with a little humor. Your grandmamma will either get better or not, according to the Lord's will. We'll make her plenty comfortable whichever way He chooses. Now, put that fresh sheet on top of her. It'll be a cooling comfort." Mrs. Garlan tossed the mourning quilt off the far side of the bed so it wouldn't be seen. That ugly, ragged old quilt would be an embarrassment.

The child was spooky, and Mrs. Garlan didn't much care for her because her eyes shifted color in the light, like a dog her husband used to have, a crazy son of a bitch if ever there was one. Noneen told her the girl saw her brother get killed, and her mama couldn't stand the sight of her while she was dealing with her grief.

That was strange. Most folks would want to hang onto the child they had left, not push her away, but they were strange people anyway, Noneen riding in that fancy car like she was Jackie Kennedy and insisting on that old-fashioned hair set when everyone else was getting perms. They may be neighbors, but that was just happenstance.

She made it a practice not to get too friendly with her clients, even the one who lived just across the highway. Of course, women just couldn't help spilling out all sorts of news when she had their heads in a sink, working out the secrets with suds that smelled of strawberries and sin. Well, she'd just have herself a looksee while they were waiting on the rescue squad to arrive. She was a good Christian woman and would do her duty to another Christian woman, but it didn't hurt none to seek out a few of them hidden sins the preacher kept speaking on.

Mrs. Garlan left the child tending to her grandmamma and wandered back out toward the parlor. Every surface in the room was covered in mother-in-law's tongue, growing prolifically toward the picture window whose curtains she'd never seen drawn apart from her own porch across the street. It looked like a jungle. Planters lined the walls, too, some two and three deep.

The parlor was not intended for visiting, but for viewing. An oak TV console held court, its cabinetry banked with bookshelves. On these shelves sat juvenile mother-in-law's tongues in a sort of nursery. Noneen didn't have any framed photographs displayed about the console like most normal folks would. Its top surface was covered in more plants and unsightly water stains where the water seeped through. It was a wonder that TV wasn't ruined.

The carpet in the parlor was an avocado green tufted wall to wall setup that Mrs. Garlan would never describe as stylish. The color clashed with the deeper, variegated greens of the cluttered plants. The path from the parlor to the kitchen beyond or the bedrooms out back was threadbare and worn, but well-vacuumed. How a house could be so cluttered and so clean simultaneously was beyond Mrs. Garland. Another set of plants flanked a small but ancient-looking bible that sat in the exact center of a coffee table that didn't quite match the wood tones of the TV console. The bible didn't appear well-read, but it was most definitely old.

Mrs. Garlan made her way into the kitchen to have a look in the drawers. What a woman keeps in her drawers reveals a lot. She kept her hooch hidden beneath the bathroom sink just for that purpose. It wouldn't do for someone to run across her alky-hol when they were rifling around for a ballpoint pen. Besides, if someone went nosing around the bathroom, she could easily explain it away as cough syrup. All the old-timers know that a hot honey and whiskey toddy will stop nighttime coughs. When it's medicinal, it doesn't count as dranking. It weren't anybody's business that she used hers as a preventative. Why, that was just smart planning.

She was just about to inspect the cabinets to see if they were as clean on the inside as on the outside when the rescue squad finally pulled up. There wasn't a hint of the grease buildup that she had such a time with at her house anywhere in this kitchen. Why, she could eat off the floors here if it weren't for all them damn mother-in-law tongues wagging all over the place. No matter, her own sorry housekeeping would be insignificant in social circles if she ever got sick, especially when folks got wind of how poor Widow High and Mighty was living behind closed doors. Mrs. Garlan smiled, the perfect hostess, as she quickly led the rescue squad back to her old friend.

"Let's get her hauled out to the wagon," said the worker after hastily checking Nonny's vital signs. "It's hot as hell in this room!"

When he saw Deborah, he let out a gasp. "You hurt, girl? You look like you've been rolling in a pig sty!"

"No, sir. Please just take care of Nonny. I'm fine," Deborah replied as she shrank back against the wall, embarrassed by her sodden gown and bare feet.

"I'll get this one in the tub, call her folks, and have them over to the hospital as soon as I can," said Mrs. Garlan, clearly reveling in responsibility.

The second rescue squad man appeared with a narrow gurney. Between the two of them, they lifted Nonny like she didn't weigh more than a mite.

"Little girl, will you please go fetch your granny's purse? She'll need it at the hospital."

As Deborah moved out of the room, he took Mrs. Garlan by the elbow. "Now, Mrs. Garlan, I don't want you to get upset, but we got a bit of a situation with the ambulance. The alternator's gone bad, and we had to come out here in, well, in Daddy's hearse. Will you keep the girl in the house until we get on our way? It's still dark yet, and I don't want her to see us putting her grandmother in the vehicle."

"Of course," replied Mrs. Garlan equably, eyes shining with what the rescue worker mistook for concern for her dear old neighbor. She wouldn't miss this for the world, but she deftly took that hideous alligator purse from the approaching girl, spun her toward the bathroom with a, "For shame to let grown men see you in your shimmies!" and wedged the pocketbook between Noneen's legs.

Just as the men were depositing Noneen into the back of the hearse, she rallied and started shouting. Her voice was slurred and hoarse, but she was clearly aware of where she was being carted and was fighting it for all she was worth. Mrs. Garlan held back a chuckle as she remembered that Old Man Pritchett died a couple of days ago. Wouldn't it be a hoot if Noneen had to ride to the hospital cozied up beside that old fart!

Bemused, she shook her head as she went to run a bath for the girl. Morning would set things to right as it always did.

"I'm going to go on back home and put on a pot of coffee so's I can call your folks. You get yourself all clean, dress in something decent, try to do something with your hair, and be ready to go to the hospital to see your grandmamma. Visitin' starts at nine. You'll want a sweater. They keep it like an icebox in there. Oh, don't you worry. They'll take good care of her, and she'll be fine. Didn't you hear her hollering at the rescue squad?"

Mrs. Garlan had Nonny's telephone and address contact book from the kitchen whatnot drawer tucked up under her elbow.

"You're not going to stay with me?" Deborah was incredulous after such a night.

"You're big enough to take care of yourself for a spell. It'll be light in an hour, so there ain't a thing to be scared of."

Mrs. Garlan pulled the bathroom door shut and made her way quickly out of the stifling house that set her teeth on edge. She aimed to temper her coffee with some liquor before she got to calling Noneen's people. Night air can bring on a cough quicker than anything.

10

Deborah

Deborah sank down into the sudsy water, careful not to let the tub overflow. Mrs. Garlan prepared the bath with dishwashing liquid when she couldn't find any proper bubble bath. A bar of soap waited on a washcloth folded daintily on the arm of the outdated porcelain tub, and a folded towel sat atop a tacky woven plastic clothes hamper for lack of a better spot in the tiny bathroom made for utilitarian function rather than luxury. The small mirror over the naked sink was already steamy when Deborah's eyes slowly closed, giving over to exhaustion and the engulfing caress of lemon-scented dishwater while the forgotten space heater in Nonny's room waged its war on the ragged quilt tossed haphazardly against its grill. The hellish night was not ready to give itself over to day just yet.

***

A piece of cotton batting, nubby and matted, caught first, smoking like a wick before erupting into flame. Wear, dry rot, and sheer age did the rest as the flames ate hungrily through the mourning quilt. In a matter of minutes, the anguish of lost children and the whitehot lust of producing more gave equal admittance to the conversion to ash.

Ashes to ashes and dust to dust, all are reduced to nothing. Even the preservation of memories is a ruse, a useless poultice on the festering wound of life. Nothing lasts forever, and sometimes it's better to let the dead stay dead. Memories can heal, but they can also cut or empower that which has no business remaining.

The mourning quilt cried as it burned, a high-pitched keening from the pent-up tears of grandmothers, mothers, and their daughters. Not just tears, but blood, hopes, secrets, and sorrows were woven through those tired fibers. As the designs melted away and the interior batting was revealed, tufts of cotton began to take flight, borne on air and ash. That uniquely human aroma—a sour melody of sweat, tears, and piss—rose in honor of its own immolation. The dust ruffle on Nonny's bed, the one effeminate feature of the otherwise staid bedroom caught next, its eyelets providing just the right amount of oxygen to feed the flames.

***

Situated so low in the tub her ears were covered by the warm water, Deborah dozed as the bubbles soaked in. She felt like she was in a cocoon of warmth, protected and held close. Her mind wandered far away to the embrace of a hollow tree, the loamy smell lulling her. The memory was so sharp, she thought she actually smelled wood, like that comforting scent of the fireplace where logs crackled while Daddy helped her and Brent skewer marshmallows on metal coat-hangers only he was strong enough to straighten.

"Deborah."

The voice was so quiet it was almost her own. She shifted in the tub and the air on her newly exposed knee roused her. The tiny bathroom was so steamy it was almost difficult to breathe. The heat, the toasty water, worry, and exhaustion combined to fill her head with cotton. Mrs. Garlan must have gotten the water too hot for her because she kept half-dreaming of an old Indian sweat lodge like on the movies, warriors staggering out to the relative safety of war.

"Deborah."

64

Her eyes snapped open. Mrs. Garlan must be waiting outside the door. The steam billowed visibly through the room. In fact, a layer of thick fog hovered above the tub. She marveled at the steam as it undulated above. It seemed to be building on itself as it rolled across the ceiling. Deborah lay in the water looking up at the steam cloud. Little pops and crackles reverberated through the muffled ocean of her ears, a faraway-fireworks show she could feel rather than see.

Her hand rose out of the water toward the steam. Her body registered the reversed temperature exchange. The air in the room was hotter than the water below, fairly sucking the moisture from her exposed arm.

"You've set the house on fire."

Whether voice, thought, or revelation it was no matter. Panic made her start to spring from the tub, but she caught herself before she could be stupid. Those poor bunk bed kids in the fire safety movie sat right up and never had a chance. Their lungs got fried before they could even yell for help.

She shifted around to her hands and knees, keeping her head low. She had to think. The bathroom was a closet with no window. The only way out was through the door, which was breathing smoke around its frame like some portal to hell. Deborah reached up and turned the cold water on full blast. Using her hands, she bailed water onto the floor to cool it down. Her nasty nightgown was balled up on the floor beside the hamper. She stretched out to grab it. *I'm not going out of here naked,* she thought. At the same time she realized the gown would likely catch fire.

"Not if you're wet," she said to the gown and brought it into the tub with her.

She floundered low in the water as she wormed into her panties, but the elastic ripped in her hurry, and she shook the underwear from her legs. The water pinked immediately with tomato juice and dirt, quickly darkening to the color of coagulated blood. Deborah reached over to the hamper and

65

brought the towel down in the water with her, too. Then she hauled the hamper itself up under the faucet. Cold water splashed her in the face as she worked furiously.

Deborah rose to her knees, sniffing the air delicately. The smoke would fill the tiny bathroom within another minute or two. She had to keep as low as possible. She wrapped the soaked towel around her waist. She would need to crawl and the towel would protect her knees for a few seconds. The nightgown, dripping with nastiness, was wrapped around her hand. She expected the door handle to be hot.

Deborah bellied her way out of the tub and onto the bathroom floor. The floor was wet from the tub overflowing, and she knew that would buy her a chance. Deborah sat back on her haunches, slipped the clothes hamper over her head for whatever protection it would afford, and reached for the doorknob.

The blast of heat hit hard, but Deborah stayed low and crawled fast through the tiny alcove leading from the bathroom into the hallway. She tossed the hamper off her head when she got to the hall. Nonny's room was in flames. The walls around her were whining, and Deborah hiked herself into a bear crawl to get more speed. The parlor was smoky but not yet aflame. Nonny's plants were waving in the heat, pointing the way toward the back door which was really on the side of the house.

Deborah looked around for something to save. People are supposed to save things in fires. She saw the ragged old Bible in its place on the coffee table and decided to grab that on her way out the door. Years of display, neglect, and Nonny's careful waxing had the thing fused to the table. Deborah yanked on it to no avail. She opened the front cover and ripped out the opening pages.

Wadding the Word of the Lord up in her fist, Deborah high-tailed it to the door, grabbed Nonny's keys from their nail on the wall, and exited the burning house. She did not forget to set the lock on her way out. She got into Nonny's Chrysler, backed it hurriedly out of the carport, and whipped the car through the backyard and all the way to the fence line at the back of the property.

The car bounced through the old field gone to seed and came to a halt well beyond the reach of the fire, cloistered by thick towers of pokeweed. That's when the nerves set in, and Deborah began shaking uncontrollably. She laid down in the front seat and hid from the flames as the sun rose, competing with Nonny's poor house for brilliance.

11

Garlan

Nigh after sunrise, Mrs. Garlan, fortified with half a pot of coffee, a strong swig of bourbon from the medicine cabinet, and the sheer joy of being the bearer of bad news over the telephone, clomped in her sturdy heels to the large mirror she kept in her garage-turned-beauty parlor to inspect herself before she went over to get Noneen's girl to meet her parents at the hospital.

Some of her best customers came from chance hospital visits and the women she fixed up while they lay sick or dying in semi-private rooms. She never charged for these visits—like a doctor making rounds—she knew she'd get paid tenfold by the grateful ladies or their next of kin, it didn't make her no nevermind, with a steady stream of business to thank her for her special kindness.

Her hair, of course, was styled perfectly in what she privately called her, "Jackie Kennedy Meets Menopause 'Do," and would be the envy of the sixty and up set she depended on for her livelihood; that along with her sorry ass husband's pension. After she got over the embarrassment of him running up under a log truck and knocking not only his own head clean off but putting some young tramp through the windshield, she come to realize she was blessed. Since nobody claimed the girl, folks assumed he must've been hauling some unlucky hitchhiker over toward Huntsville. She knew better, but didn't let on in her grief. She thanked the son of a bitch every third of the month when his check arrived like clockwork. He'd been a much better husband since that wreck.

"Fit to kill!" she smiled with the satisfaction of knowing she'd kept herself up decades beyond most women her age, even if she was a little plump. She'd rather be filled out than dried up anyhow. She gave herself one more healthy fogging of hairspray and stepped out for what promised to be an exciting day.

She smelled smoke as soon she was out the door and cursed at her neighbor Hellfire Whittaker for burning leaves before the sun even got up good. That man burned more leaves than you could shake a stick at. It was his goal in life to keep a pall of smoke over his house. He said it kept the skeeters down. Once she got her car turned around, though, she saw that the smoke poured out of the house across the highway.

"That damn girl's done set the house afire!" Mrs. Garlan slammed the gear into park and waddled as fast as her clunky heels and pencil skirt would let her back into the beauty parlor to call the rescue squad for the second time in a matter of hours.

"Hope your fire truck is runnin' this morning. Y'all get on back here in a hurry!"

The rescue squad loved a good fire and would be on the way in a matter of minutes. Their voices got all excited on the scanner she liked to listen to when she couldn't sleep. The drunks and crazies all came out on Saturday nights. The scanner on a North Alabama Saturday night was more entertaining by far than any program on the TV. This being early Sunday morning, Mrs. Garlan knew it'd take the squad a little longer to get the truck going. They were groggy from the regular Saturday night antics and half-hung over from their own.

She sped back across the highway and parked in the front yard so the fire truck would be able to pull up in the driveway. Her hands gripped the wheel as she peered toward the smoking house, looking for a sign of the girl. As she was wont to do when in some sort of pickle, she spoke aloud.

"Now, I left that little girl alone in the house. I ought not to have done that. If she gets burnt up, it'll be my fault. I won't be able to show my face. If I get hold of her before the rescue squad

69

gets here, I'll be a hero. Ladies will be lined up out my parlor door."

Mrs. Garlan wiggled out of the car and marched up the front porch steps. She noticed the No Solisiting sign by the door and harrumphed before knocking.

"Debbie? Little Debbie? You in there?" she called before opening the door herself and charging inside.

It was difficult to see as she shouted for the girl, first heading toward the kitchen, then pivoting toward the back of the house. The heat was so intense and the smoke so choking she became disoriented before she even realized she was in trouble. The child was nowhere to be found. Flames engulfed the hallway and rushed like a torrent above her, racing for the tepid morning air streaming through the front door now hidden in smoke. She was turned around. She couldn't find the door. She had to get out, damn the kid.

Mrs. Garlan dropped to her knees, gasping to catch her breath as the smoke gagged her. Those godforsaken houseplants were swaying, writhing in the heat like black tongues reaching for her. She was in a room full of snakes, spitting venom at her as their innards steamed. She crawled, but the parlor seemed long as a football field and narrow as a coffin all at once.

The plants surrounded her as the fire roared above, having its way with the attic before it closed ranks on the jungle below. The noxious odor of roasting mother-in-law's tongue seared her nostrils, a vegetable smell of earthy rot, seeping into her pores and permeating the room in a nimbus of boiled cabbage as her own blood began to cook. She lost consciousness before her Jackie O. pouf ignited and disintegrated instantly in its hairspray caul. Her scalp barely singed, Mrs. Garlan succumbed to the smoke, as the legion of plants hissed in protest, and died.

Moments later, the rescue squad returned bleary-eyed in a blaze of sirens. "Why does everything happen in either the dead of night or the crack of dawn?" CJ Jeffers mused as he drained off the dregs of his black coffee and tossed the Styrofoam cup in the yard.

Littering didn't make no difference in a fire; everything's tore up to hell anyhow. The front door was open, but the old bag who called them in wasn't around. Neither was that girl who stayed behind when he hauled her grandma off just a-hollerin' in the back of his daddy's hearse. Now, that was gonna be one of those stories he'd be tellin' for years!

Boy, that church lady cussed a blue streak all the way to the hospital. It was all slurry on account of her having had a stroke, and she was so wrought up she was likely to stroke out again before they could get her to the hospital. She made it, though, and now she's gonna find out her house done burnt to the ground. They always burnt to the ground, especially the houses out a piece like this one.

CJ sent Buddy around back to find the well and spigots. Buddy Sheffield was a distant cousin and his best friend since fifth grade. They ran the roads together all through high school and were still at it as a proud part of the volunteer rescue squad. When they weren't chasing fires and hurt folks, Buddy made good money as a mechanic over at the gas station, and CJ was taking business classes at the junior college so he could "amount to something" as his daddy liked to preach.

CJ dressed quickly in the flame retardant worksuit, threw on his helmet, and grabbed the ax. He tromped up the front porch and into the burning house just in case. He wasn't two good steps inside when he found Mrs. Garlan sprawled on the floor. He quickly surveyed the room for the girl, and hoped she was out back with Buddy. The roof was going to collapse any minute and he was already roasting in that suit. He grabbed Mrs. Garlan by a hefty ankle and dragged her out onto the porch.

"Buddy!" he hollered. Buddy came running around the corner with a garden hose, dropped it, and helped CJ haul Mrs. Garlan out of harm's way. Several other volunteers whipped into the driveway, having heard about the emergency on their

71

scanners. A house fire on a Sunday morning was not to be missed.

"Is she dead?" asked Buddy, with a tinge of excitement in his voice.

"As a doornail. Who would've known the hairdresser was bald as a goose?" CJ shook his head and shuddered. "God, I don't wanna grow old. Go get the sheet, and radio for Daddy. He's got work to do. Is the girl out back? It's too far gone to go back in there."

"No. Damn."

"Damn."

12

Isom

"Holy shit, she's done set the house on fire!" Isom Ballard exclaimed as he whipped the sleek Lincoln Continental Town Car into the driveway. He picked his way through a sea of pickups and a sorry ass Pinto held together with Bond-O just as the carport roof collapsed on nothing. He looked around the yard-turned-parking lot and didn't see Caro's mama's Chrysler.

The firemen, most of them looked like high school boys skipping out on Sunday School, let out a spontaneous cheer before being shushed by a uniformed fellow who didn't look much older. A couple of them worked limp garden hoses, wetting down the yard around the house so the fire wouldn't spread or get up in the surrounding trees. Clearly, they were letting the house burn itself out.

The bonfire atmosphere, though, was subdued by the sheeted lump on the ground up under the sprawling oak tree. Isom started when he saw that, but immediately assessed the lump was too large to be his daughter. Besides, Deb was small for her age. She'd always be Little Debbie, no matter how Caro harped on the more formal Deborah. His girl was too runtish for such a stout name. She took after him in stature—he'd been called wormy as a kid and had to fight his way to respect ever since, one way or another—and she took after him that way, too.

Isom suddenly realized he missed her during the interminable spring and summer after the accident. He barely thought about her between trying to keep himself, Caro, and the business from joining Brent in the grave. She had her mother's eyes, the eyes that had mesmerized him fifteen years ago with their depth. Their eyes would shift color according to the light and mood. He used to piss Caro off on purpose just to see those eyes shift, an aphrodisiac if ever there was one. But Caro's eyes saw right past him now, dull and bloodshot from grief and lack of sleep. He'd turned the corner on it, learned to move within its choking presence. Regret would be an ever-present shackle, but Brent's ghost finally turned him loose, or maybe he set Brent's ghost free. Caro was still hanging on.

Isom Ballard strode out of his huge frigate of a car, ready to take charge of these boys playing at fire. He made a direct line for the uniformed fellow who was pacing nervously out under the oak a few feet from the shrouded figure.

"Isom Ballard," he stated as way of introduction without bothering to wait for the volunteer's reply. He was probably some grease monkey anyhow, out for the thrill of a siren.

"This dump is my wife's folks'."

Ballard always stopped a few feet out from men he was talking to because he didn't like having to obviously look up at them like some little prick begging attention. "Her mama's at the hospital, and her mama's car's gone. Who the hell is that?"

"It's the neighbor lady from across the highway," replied CJ. "Daddy's—uh, the coroner—is on the way. She was my mama's hairdresser. I bet Mama never knew the old lady was bald as a goose." He knelt down on the far side of the corpse and adjusted the tarp so nothing would show. It was hard to look at dead folks.

"Garlan the name? Yep. She called us in the middle of the night to let us know my mother-in-law'd had a stroke," Isom glanced nonplussed at the sheeted mound and murmured, "Serves the old bag right for nosing around." Then he returned his eyes to the rescue boy. "My wife's at the hospital and I'm here to get my daughter. Where is she?"

CJ took off his squad cap, ran his hand through his slickened hair, and began to wring the cap. He swallowed hard before he

74

spoke. "Well, sir. It…, it was just too far gone by the time we got here," CJ paused again. He could take adults dying in accidents. They had their chance to live their lives. Kids, though, tore him up. "We believe your little girl is still in the house."

"Unless one of you ignorant, do-gooder, flame jockeys stole the damn Chrysler out of the carport while the house burned down around it, she ain't in the house! Stupid shits. Who's your damn daddy, son?"

CJ stood up. Damn it, he hadn't noticed the missing car. Neither had poor old Mrs. Garlan. Steep price to pay, and Ballard barely gave her a second glance. She died trying to save his daughter, for Christ sakes.

He could show this arrogant asshole just how ignorant he was if he had to. He might be wiry, but he had a good six inches on Ballard. Whipping the sucker's ass on a Sunday morning over a dead body, though, would hurt his mama's heart and be a disrespect to Mrs. Garlan. CJ pushed his anger down as far as he could.

"My daddy's Chuck Lawson, and I ain't your son. I'm a grown-ass man."

"Aw, hell. I should've known. Can't nothing happen in this God-forsaken county without a goddamned Lawson being all up in it." Isom turned on his heel and stomped back toward what was left of the carport. The other rescue squad fellows avoided eye contact, making themselves appear busy while they waited for things to cool down enough to recover a body that was not to be found.

He didn't think Debbie would have the gall to drive off too far with a house afire. He made a wide berth around the corner of the carport, which was smoldering in the morning sun like it was in some sort of competition with the latest heat wave. Sure enough, tire tracks led off across the back field all gone chest high to weed and briars. A little rise in the land hid the car almost perfectly.

Isom trudged along the beat-down track and wished he'd worn boots instead of the loafers he'd slipped on in Caro's panic to get to her ailing mother. They both assumed Debbie would be at the hospital with her grandmother. It pissed him off to have to drive another fifteen minutes to fetch her, and it pissed him off even more to hear the scanner at the emergency room desk alert everybody and their brother of a fire at Caro's mama's place.

Caro was distracted by all that was going on with her mama and for once, he was glad of her training as a nurse. He wasn't sure he could stand the embarrassment of another of Caro's full-on drawing spells that was sure to come if she thought Debbie was burnt up, especially coming so hard upon her mama's stroke.

He never doubted his daughter's safety. Hell, she probably set the fire. He'd want to burn the place down, too, if he had to live with that old hag all summer. There was no telling what kind of religious hocus-pocus had been brainwashed into his daughter while they were trying to work through Brent's death. He and Caro were both so beside themselves it seemed like the best idea at the time. She needed to be away from all the sorrow. They needed her to be away from them. He realized once again that he'd missed Debbie and that it may have been a mistake to send her away. She was already weird as hell. Maybe the summer hadn't screwed her up too bad.

But now, there'd be another dead person to deal with. What the hell kind of crazy-ass would leave a kid alone in the night after her grandmother got carted off to the hospital? Maybe she hadn't. Maybe she'd stayed at the house with Debbie and that's what got her killed. Why would Debbie save herself and leave the old lady trapped inside, though? That didn't make sense. It must have happened some other way.

Isom topped the rise in the field. The morning dew was burning off faster than the house behind him. He could almost see it evaporating. It was going to be another scorcher, and he regretted wearing his khakis and button-down. On a normal Sunday morning, he'd be in trunks, reading the paper by the pool built in anticipation of an insurance payoff. It was so new he could still smell the red clay under the mound of pine chips and dwarf azaleas he'd chosen to landscape around it. It was an oasis, certainly the biggest backyard pool in Scottsboro, and by-God, he was going to enjoy it, because he had by-God earned it.

Brent was gone, but that didn't mean his life had to be over. That didn't mean Caro's life had to be over, even if she did rant and accuse him of building a swimming pool on the blood of their son, swearing to not so much as dip a toe in that bloodied water. She'd come around in time. It didn't mean that Debbie's life had to be over either, and it was high time they quit punishing her for the sin of being at home when Brent ran that cart up under the truck. That made about as much sense as punishing the truck for being parked in the driveway. It was an accident, pure and simple. The poor kid just had more than her share of accidental deaths.

Maybe she didn't know about this latest one. Isom approached the car, which was still running. What the hell was she doing, sitting in the car while the house burned down? He looked inside the window and saw her curled up on the front seat, a football stadium cushion pillowed under her head. Barefoot, bare-assed, and streaked with grime, she slept.

Isom stood mesmerized. Her hair poked out in tufts and her skin was rosy despite the muck. The curve of her naked hip promised a blossoming almost at any moment. He thought of marble. His sleeping daughter was sleek, a perfect combination of the best of Caro and his compact strength. She was the most beautiful creature he'd ever seen.

She must have sensed his presence. She shifted; and in that movement, he caught a glimpse of hair, blonde and downy, between her legs. His amazement was quickly covered up by embarrassment. He shouldn't be looking on his daughter—his beautiful, safe daughter—in this way. It was too private, too precious.

77

The spell broken, Isom moved quickly to the other side of the car and tried the door. It was locked. He tapped on the window until she awoke, bleary-eyed and grasping for a sodden towel. He was already taking off his button-down as she opened the door, a blast of heat emanating from the car.

"Daddy?" she asked as if she didn't quite recognize him.

"What have you done now? Are you hurt? The house is burned to the ground and you out here sleeping half-naked in the car. Put this on!"

He was speaking raggedly as he helped her into his shirt, chastising and hugging all at the same time. Even though he was not a big man, his shirt swallowed her. He wanted to swallow her, keep her safe, lock her away in a tower from a world whose cruel underbelly could never slide over her again.

Sitting beside her, he held her as she shivered despite the heat. The vehicle was stifling. As he stretched over her to cut the ignition and grab the keys, his loafers crushed some paper littering the floorboard. He kicked the crinkly pages up under the seat to get them out of his way. Isom couldn't get her out of there fast enough.

"Daddy," she repeated over and over as whatever the hell happened to her in the night wracked her with sobs.

"We're going home, Little Debbie. We're going home."

He scooped her up and began the long walk back through the overgrown field toward the remains of the house. He had his girl, and he vowed not to let her go again. Her soured breath mingled with the sweat on his neck as she nestled into the sudden comfort his embrace offered. It was a starved-for comfort that she sucked in ravenously.

He had himself under control by the time he got her back to the yard proper. He managed to get her into his Town Car while avoiding any possibility of her seeing the mound that was Mrs. Garlan sacked up under the tree. He was never gladder of springing for the extra fifteen hundred dollars to have the windows heavily tinted.

78

If one of those dumbasses watching the fire burn so much as looked sidelong at his nubile daughter, he might explode. The house didn't matter. It was an eyesore before it burned. The old bag in the bag—he almost chuckled at his own pun—didn't matter. Served her right for being nosy, the old bitch.

Come to think of it, Caro didn't matter much either. Not anymore. That girl, his girl, laid out on the cool leather backseat, skin so soft it felt like butter under his fingertips, and wrapped in his designer shirt, she mattered.

PART TWO

MOTHER

Atlantic Crossing 178+

13

Maisie

The fetor of smoke, roasted flesh, and horse sweat mingled with the evaporating dew rising off her cape as her daughter rested snug in the balmy warmth beneath. The plodding gait of the mount lulled her, too, and she found herself nodding as the morning sun rose beyond the distant tree line. She willed herself not to look back, not to give any indication of escape.

Constant wiping had removed most of the blood from her hands, but her nails were black with it. She scratched at the horse's hide, tickling up the bristly hairs to tease the dried gore away. She pleasured in the thought of the former Lord Clemenceau being plucked from her life as readily as this detritus from 'neath her fingernails. He was a memory to be wiped away, to slough off her body and be trodden into this endless shit-piled road.

L'Arbol had almost been in her grasp. Renny's place had almost been assured. She managed the properties, kitchens, nursery, and yes, even his bed better than any highborn weakling or child-bride he brought to his wasted legacy ever could. If only she'd bore him a son—bastard no matter—fortune might have taken a happier turn. He treated her as a bauble to be had or put away at his whim. He kept her in a gilded cage only to exchange it for a prison of a coarser kind. For that, he paid.

All that remained of *L'Arbol* for Maisie Sessile was a smattering of acorns collected during her lying-in before Renny's unfortunate birth. They became a sort of talisman as she plotted the necessary death of Clemenceau. She counted them out much as she counted out the dreaded sweetmeats that heralded his arrival, and consequently, his demise.

Her only regret was the requirement of Renny delivering the death-blow. Oh, the girl sucked on hatred just as her father whet his cruel appetites with marzipan, savoring the flavor of her ire; she had his penchant for recompense when dealt falsely. Maisie doubted the girl would lose her compunction even if she knew the throat beneath her sharpened point was the selfsame who begat her. Perhaps the girl surmised the truth with that sharp verity children often possess, but Maisie never revealed the paternity of her "foundling." Renny accepted their turning-out with a brooding anger Maisie stealthily managed to turn toward Clemenceau during their mutual imprisonment.

The surprise in this equation rode steadily ahead of her, a lead rope connecting the party as they made their way toward Calais and the mystery of the Americas. Beauchene, or her beloved husband Randall Clemence as they agreed to identify themselves henceforth, rode with the straight-backed ease of a man well acquainted with hours in the saddle.

She watched as his shoulders and haunches moved with the fluid motion of the horse. She detected confidence in his stance but no haughtiness in his demeanor. This was a man who knew not caprice, but one who would remain steadfast in righting what he perceived wrong 'twere it in his power. He proclaimed himself her champion, and now her husband and would fully expect requital for escorting her away from the clutches of the lord of *L'Arbol*. She would have to unseat him eventually, of this she was sure. For now, however, he could prove quite useful in ensuring the safety of the child on what would likely be a most unhospitable journey.

Maisie could smell the salt on the air long before the walls of Calais appeared in the distance. Renny stirred, emerging from her mother's cape much as a turtle thrusts its head from the shell, eyes blinking in the brilliance of the day.

"Maman, are those the masters?" She pointed toward the city though no ships were yet to be seen.

"Patience, child. We'll be aboard 'ere long."

Maisie sounded at ease although her heart raced. These next few hours would decide their fate. Either this *family* would set sail into obscurity or be tried and most certainly convicted for the death of Lord Clemenceau. Forsooth, he would not be mourned, but justice would be served despite the injustices he served her and would surely deal to Renny had they given him time for her to come of age. They would all escape together or hang together. It was as simple as that.

She reached into her pocket and pulled out the wooden ship Beauchene carved as they readied themselves for this fearful passage. Carefully, she opened its secret hinge and shook the emptied vials of poison out of the hold. She tossed one vial into the thicket by the wayside. The other she palmed while the horses moved onward another good quarter hour. She considered casting it into the sea but chose not to risk its discovery should they be searched quayside. Gently, nonchalantly, Maisie dropped it into a wheel rut to be crushed by an oxcart filled with dung if her hopes be granted.

From her bosom she pulled the leather baglet containing coinage and acorns. She would take *L'Arbol* with her and she would give at least some semblance of *L'Arbol* to her daughter, its rightful heir. Into the hull of the miniature barque she stuffed the acorns. She murmured a little prayer with each one.

Maisie was not sure if she actually believed in God, at least not the one the priests extolled with their mysterious Latin, vestments, and guilt while being nothing more than base men beneath. If a God-dealt justice would allow her to procure it with her own hands and secure it for her daughter, she would willingly pay the soul-price. She'd paid enough of herself to that damnable Clemenceau that any god worth his salt would grant her absolution for this vengeance.

Beauchene guided his mount into a fallow field, Maisie's tethered ride following close behind. He dismounted, set a quick picket, and helped his new wife and daughter down to stretch their legs whilst the horses fed. His quick eye followed Maisie's glance back toward the road.

"The best place to hide, *ma chérie*, is in plain sight. It shall be far easier to pass yourself off as a country wife than as a lady. Truth be told, you'd have done that readily enough had the folk of *L'Arbol* not already known you as a kitchen wench. I should think you would have succeeded 'twere it another manor," he said with eyes sparkling. He was clearly enjoying this adventure, even with the possibility of his own neck being stretched if apprehended by Clemenceau's men.

"We need to freshen," Maisie replied.

"You'll find a brook a few hundred paces east, milady," he responded with an affected flourish of his hand. "I'll bring the mounts along shortly, so that you and the girl can wash a bit o' grime away in peace. It will be as pleasant as a holiday before we get stowed in the hold of *The Praying Mantis*."

Maisie took Renny by the hand and led her toward the brook. Renny's hands bore no evidence of her bloody deed, but her nails were chewed to the nub. Maisie quailed at the thought of her daughter sucking the blood of the beast her father, but she quickly set the thought aside. The hem of Renny's shift, however, was soiled with what would not pass as mud upon more than a cursory glance. A thorough scrubbing should wash away the last traces of their iniquity as surely as the fire had removed the last traces of his cruelty.

"Maman," asked Renny. "will the guardsman be my father?"

"Yes, *ma doux*," she responded without hesitation. "He will guide us to a new life where we shan't be kept like pets. He is our vouchsafe into a new world where you shall have the opportunity to be the lady I was denied through treachery."

"Then I shall love him. But, Maman, if he betrays us, I could do it again. 'Twas simple, really." Renny's voice was almost

86

melodic as she spoke of killing a man, almost eager. Her nonchalance was unnerving.

Maisie searched her daughter's face, trying to plumb the depths of her guilt through her eyes. She detected none. The child's eyes shifted from blue to green under the scrutiny, and Maisie took the proud little chin in her hand to gain Renny's undivided attention.

"We must never speak of that time again, my poppet. To do so may bring great harm to either, or both, of us. We must promise to lock that deed away in the past, bury it deep within our hearts. We shall away, but the world is not broad enough to escape what we've taken if ever we're recognized. Shall we make a solemn promise?"

"May I have a kitten to take along at sea?" the girl countered.

"*D'accord.*" Maisie was surprised at the ease with which her daughter's silence would be purchased.

"Then I shall promise never to think on it again!" Renny fairly leaped in excitement.

Beauchene neared the pair, horses in hand. From a distance, they appeared the perfect tableau of a sylvan family enjoying a high summer's day. Renny skittered up the bank of the brook and effected a perfect curtsey. "*Bonjour, Papa! Je m'appelle* Renae Clemence." With that, she embraced the man whose eyebrows raised at the sudden affection; then, she skipped merrily through the tall grass, stopping to gather flowering weeds.

"Are you gathering those for your maman, child?" he asked, infected by her sudden energy.

"Of course not. They're for me! Maman can gather her own as she wishes," the girl replied with a laugh. She'd be pretty if not for her odd hair, but it would surely grow, and a good cap could cover the strangeness in the meantime. She would bloom into a lasting beauty, much like her mother.

"I suppose that makes me Randall Clemence henceforth," he said to Maisie as she gathered the outerwear they placed by the brook. She looked back at the water flowing clear and strong.

87

That and a child's promise washed away the past. It was all too simple. Randall handed Maisie up from the bank. "My sweet Cecille?" he asked with a glint of amusement in his eye.

"Haven't I ever been?" she simpered.

"She will be true?" he nodded toward the frolicking child.

"'Tis already forgotten. You'll want to procure a kitten before we board, Papa, and you'll have gained a daughter's devotion."

"How about of a wife?"

"That, of course, remains to be discovered, but I warn you. You may have made a harder bargain than you recognize."

"Indeed."

14

Cecille

"I shall not breathe until France dips below the horizon," proclaimed Madame Cecille Clemence watching the eddies swirl in the ship's wake as she leaned over the rail of *The Praying Mantis*.

"But, Maman, you must breathe to speak as you are now," prattled Renae at her mother's side. The girl required no time at all to gain her sea legs and colored appealingly with the salt air. In fact, were it not for hair that seemed to grow in happenstance tufts rather than proper ringlets as well as those eyes whose hue shifted according to light and whim, she might be considered beautiful.

Cecille, on the other hand, felt queasy from the moment she stepped aboard, and the bark rocked against its moorings. She chewed on a tasteless hard biscuit to help settle her stomach. The very thought of the dripping honeyed cakes she so often baked in her girlhood at *L'Arbol* made these ship's biscuits all the more vile, but Randall assured her they would give her a stomach for the sea ere long.

It was difficult to think of him as husband, but if their ruse were to succeed, a husband he must be in both appearance and practice. The ship's interior walls appeared so thin, the sound of their coupling would fire the imaginations of the men in the adjacent berths. She trusted the hull was hewn of much stronger timber, for who knew how they would be tossed about the sea on their seven-weeks' journey.

As she and Renae were the only females of consequence aboard, the little family had been afforded the second-best cabin on the *Mantis*, as the three-master was commonly called. Her captain, Bonneval, a peevish man who vaguely resembled a rodent, was a portrait of manners and practicality. The walls were thin enough for her to overhear him explaining to her husband the utility of keeping a brace of whores in the ship's hold for a bit of recreation on the long journey to the Antilles.

He pledged to keep them well out of sight and admonished Randall not to allow his wife and daughter to walk the decks unaccompanied, especially at night. A turnabout could be treacherous in more ways than one. Of course, the captain went on, the whores would be available for M. Clemence's sport per his request, as they were providing their services in kind for passage to the isles. The men chuckled amicably, already fast friends.

"Come, Renae, let's get below and see what we can do to make that tiny cabin hospitable," directed Cecille.

"Maman, did you marry with the kind guardsman?"

"Hist!" Cecille seethed. "You will do well, *petite mademoiselle*, to call him Papa or we may all be undone. We are not yet out of danger, but I'll warrant we will not be pursued across the sea. We mayn't be pursued at all, but you must remember that if we are apprehended, it was your hand that delivered death unto that beast. I shan't be able to protect you from the hangman's noose, so this secret you must keep. Do you understand, child?"

"'Twas easy, Maman," the girl repeated. "Were it to do over, I would not hesitate to destroy him again. He used you cruelly. He kept us as pets. I shan't forgive him."

"There's nothing left but ash to forgive, but you must never confess these things aloud again. Let me see the tiny ship I gave you."

Renae pulled the plaything from her pocket and proffered it to her mother. Cecille opened the latch and shook out a pair of plump acorns.

"Do you see these seeds? They become towering oaks, but only when planted and nurtured over a great deal of time. They are your legacy, all that remains of your rightful inheritance which I now understand we must leave forever if we are to survive. I wished to take all of *L'Arbol*, but that is not to be. You, Renae, must grow them when you reach fertile ground. That may be some years hence, when you are a woman and I am gone. If you must confess, whisper your soul-secrets into the hull, here; it's a truer shrift than any you shall encounter in a church."

Cecille took an acorn, kissed it, and placed it back in the bauble. "I'll begin." She held the ship to her mouth and breathed her name, her true name, inside, never to be spoken again. Renae, her Renny, looked at her with steel gray eyes as she held another acorn to her lips.

"The beast was my father?" she asked.

"*Oui, enfante.*"

"That makes my vengeance ever so sweeter." She kissed the acorn prettily and placed it in the hold. "I shall use this ship, Maman, as a keeper of secrets just as you direct. It is a sepulcher of sorts, is it not? Confessions, though, I have none. I quite enjoyed watching fear fill his eyes."

With that, Renae sealed the hull and dropped the toy ship back into her pocket. Cecille choked down another wave of nausea, took her daughter by the arm, and led her below.

They never spoke of Lord Clemenceau again. Nor did Cecille lay eyes on the handheld sepulcher again. Renae tucked it away. Whether meant to sustain life or be borne from death, the acorns of *L'Arbol* remained sealed inside, inexorably grinding against one another through the trials of a lifetime, perhaps many lifetimes.

Cecille wished she could see the acorns planted in their new home, but the climate would vary as surely as the climate of their lives had reached yet another season. The winter of her life was over, to be supplanted by an endless summer. She would shed the new man from herself as soon as they arrived at the Antilles, just as one sheds a cloak in the brightness of a new day.

There was no happiness in it, though, and little hope. The island heat Captain Bonneval described would just be a precursor of the fires of hell that awaited her, not for killing, but for awakening the lust for pain in her daughter's eyes. She saw it clearly in that moment on deck, although she thought she had squelched these adumbrations in the child's demeanor during their entrapment. Renae never resembled the beast more.

15

Bonneval

Captain Bonneval wiped his hands on his breeches quickly before extending them in greeting to the *Mmes*. Clemence. Despite the weather or his mood, he could all but wring sweat from his digits, which were undersized in comparison to his girth. His feet were undersized, too, blazoning a similarity in his other appendage which, to his shame, was quite accurate. He detected recognition in the mother's eyes when she first came aboard his bark but hid his own immediate intuition that this family was nothing of the sort.

Her quill hovered, hesitating before dipping into the inkwell and scrawling her name in a fine script onto his ship's log. They wouldn't be the first to sail under assumed monikers; and, as long as they kept him in coin, he frankly cared not. The passage was a challenging one, especially without provisions, which the forcibly becalmed family failed to carry on board. His eyes gleamed with the thought of the family disembarking with considerably lighter pockets than they boarded, for he would provide for them handsomely.

What intrigued him most was the girl. She held the look of an animal trapped, eyes darting and even seeming to change color with the light, like one of the chameleons he looked forward to the pleasure of tasting roasted on a spit once they reached the Antilles. Her eyes were almost reptilian in that they were devoid of the passion and silliness he had seen in other girls near her size. This girl, Renae as they called her, was on the cusp of blossoming, her breasts tight little buds yet to be awakened.

Perhaps this passage would provide the diversion of a different sport.

The girl struck his fancy, to be sure. He found himself thinking of her strange tufted hair as he sampled the pair of whores who would pay rather handsome fees for this passage spent largely on their backs, yet would emerge in a new world smartly dressed in new frocks with matching parasols, the very likenesses of ladies. This arrangement worked to the benefit of all.

Almost ironically, the plainer lasses would often find a place serving the already established ladies of *Beausejour*, many of whom shared histories whose stories were curiously devoid of the tales of their journey overseas. The more spirited girls, the ones who would gladly continue in their service to traders, would book passage again on to the Port of New Orleans or its eastern sister, the Port of Mobile. The captain knew not—nor cared not—what became of them once he received his "handling fee" quayside.

The crossing was demanding on the women in particular, both physically and in spirit. They were fortunate to sail on a bark whose captain took special pains to ensure their well-being. He employed a shrewd purser, a Jew called Ephraim, who vouchsafed the passengers' coin and kept a modest ship's store where the occasional lady on board—or more frequently whore—could simply sign her name. At the end of the voyage, the travelers would find their purses significantly lighter, but not so much as to perceive they had been robbed.

Captain Bonneval depended on the letters the women who could write penned once they reached the balmy paradise of La Desirade, of whose passage back to the continent Ephraim also kept a careful account. Whores were easy enough to ship, but genteel ladies were much more lucrative cargo willing to pay quite dearly to keep their indiscretions during the two-month's sail in close quarters quiet. The women of this transparent family, Clemence as they wished to be known, fell somewhere between

94

the categories. The mother was almost certainly the learned mistress of someone of means, if not standing. Likely, the purse she carried, vouchsafed by her *husband*, was ill-gotten. It would be an intriguing crossing, indeed.

The final leg of the voyage, with the Antilles rising at last from the seemingly endless ocean and alight in the glow of the setting sun was Ephraim's cue for fleecing the ladies and whores alike. The aft deck housed the most luxurious item aboard the *Mantis*: a copper bathing tub. Woven mats formed makeshift walls for privacy, although the women tittered at the singular experience of sky bathing beneath the tropic sun.

After almost two months of fresh water rations, the females were ripe for a good scrubbing. Ephraim kept a treasure chest of soap cakes in lavender, rose petal, rosemary, and lye. For a nominal fee, Ephraim offered a shaven sliver, nearly diaphanous, along with a teakwood scraper. Whether the women afforded first or second waters, the salty baths provided refreshed bodies and outlooks afore disembarking.

The *miraculous* appearance of the copper tub was still many weeks away and the untested passengers aboard were in the throes of greening their sea legs, as Captain Bonneval cheerily called the greensickness that so often came with sailing. Chamber pots in the corners of the hold brimmed with filth, for in addition to the moneyed family he quartered handsomely and the brace of whores bunking handily, a dozen Anabaptists shipped themselves as cargo. Bonneval did not particularly care for Anabaptists, but as they paid the cargo rate and brought aboard provisions, he shipped them.

He considered outfitting the *Mantis* to transport African slaves to the Port of New Orleans. His experience with carrying human cargo, however, kept him in check despite the potential earnings. Even with provisions, passage in the hold was miserable. The dank air bred contagion. Rare was a sailing that did not end in a watery grave for some passenger of this sort. The stench became almost unbearable. Bonneval imagined the people of La Desirade could smell their arrival before they could sight the ship's mark. He simply couldn't stomach the idea of policing Africans making the passage in chains and wished not to gamble on profits when other less odious goods could make his way smooth.

Oddly, the Clemence girl showed no ill effects from riding the billows. Her parents—of the mother he was sure but she bore no resemblance to the father whatsoever—were more typical. Both were confined to the cabin within arm's grasp of buckets the girl must be draining out the porthole every few hours, for she did not emerge from the cabin. She must be growing a-weary of the constant care, constant putrescence, and constant moaning of her seasick parents. An invitation to sup would be most welcome, he surmised, and provide opportunity to press the girl.

16

Cecille

After four interminable days, Cecille could finally stomach more than a sip of tepid water and hard biscuit. Whatever idyllic evenings imagined by Clemence with his knowledgeable wife—be it fact or fantasy, did it truly matter?—aboard *The Praying Mantis*, they lie curdling in the chamber pots beside their shared bunk. The greensickness left them both weakened and feverish, dependent on Renae to sponge their foreheads with cool seawater, spoon broth that would come at exorbitant price Cecille was sure, and portage those brimming chamber pots across the room to dump out of the porthole. The girl kept the porthole shuttered the rest of the time, so that it became difficult to separate night from day, dream from lucidity, past from present.

Beauchene lay insensate beside her, and she reminded herself he was now Clemence and she his wife. Renae accepted the lie readily enough. Anything else a child may believe was pacified by the tiny grey kitten the guardsman presented in a handsome wicker cage to her daughter. She reminded herself again the man, their savior, passed as a smithy rather than a guardsman. She hoped his skills would not be called for on the bark, for the ruse simply accounted for his size.

He appeared weak now, scruff sprouting from his chin as he dozed fitfully. A speck of vomit lingered in the corner of his mouth. Cecille wiped it away with her sleeve, lest the sight of it set her off again. Her body could not possible have anything left to retch, but a sudden roll of the ship provoked angry waves of nausea as if her humours were themselves storm-tossed. She shivered under the thin, scratchy blanket and sidled up even closer to Clemence on the narrow bunk. In her misery, she cared more for what heat the man could offer than awakening his senses.

If he felt half as poorly as she, the lessons he wished her to impart were far from at hand. Her head resting on his shoulder, Cecille watched her daughter reading by a coal lantern. It must be evening. She pondered where the girl obtained a volume, for they brought no book in their hasty flight. Someone rapped on the door, Renae rose, trimmed the lantern, smoothed her hair and skirts, glanced with disgust at the chamber pots, and left the sickroom.

"My young mademoiselle," intoned the unmistakably oily voice of the captain.

"Renny?" Cecille called in a cracked voice. The girl stopped short.

"Why, Maman, you must be quite ill to use my nursery name. I'm off to fetch you and Papa some broth and some cream for Bourrasque. He cries without end. Try to rest now."

The boat pitched again as Renae closed the door. Cecille lay helpless in the darkness with stomach rolling as she thought of the unexpected kindness of Captain Bonneval placing Renae in his charge.

Finally, the greensickness relented. Both Cecille and Randall regained their strength apace, with Cecille's spells ebbing to a vague greening during their morning turnabouts on deck. With Randall's hand constantly steadying her at the elbow, she knew he would call her to account ere long. Renae accompanied them along the way, always with her book in hand. A humid breeze whispered its secrets amongst the sails, who responded in languid ripples punctuated by the crackle of sailcloth, as the wind toyed with the flag on the mizzenmast.

"I shall know you tonight," said Randall as he brushed a strand of silver loosed by the breeze behind Cecille's ear. She nodded assent. She saw no gain in playing coy and rather warmed to his guiding hand. The greensickness altered her perspective, and with each passing day, they sailed closer to a new beginning.

'Twas a beginning Clemence somehow fit into. She hadn't the heart or the means to kill another man and figured her luck to already be played. Anything beyond was to invite disaster. It was not lost on her that this man granted her clemency, a pun she felt surely to be the handiwork of God, to whom she found herself praying once again. Perhaps He was making amends for her ill-use.

17

Renae

The kitten's incessant yowling was a source of irritation even for Renae, who grew bored with the novelty of a baby animal and left poor Bourrasque largely neglected in its wickered cage. She would take it out long enough for Maman to tip its litter in the piss pot, secure it in her curtained bunk, and watch it paw madly at the rats scrabbling within the wall boards.

Renae imagined the rats running next to her head to be enormous, large enough to destroy Bourrasque if ever they became locked in battle. Her bunk was aloft over the porthole, thus blocking out light during the day, so she preferred to stay below, even when Maman and Papa were felled by the greensickness. Situated beneath her bunk—clearly designed for a ship's boy—was a tiny *escritoire* and chair. It was in the drawer of this *escritoire* she found the volume that saved her from the horrors of her mother and new father's sickness. That and the discovery she made in her upper bunk.

Shadowy melancholy, her mother and newfound father's unceasing regorgement, and the irascible kitten's mewling gnawed at Renae's nerves, so she did not notice the sliding wall hidden behind the curtain of her bunk for several days. In fact, when another volume first appeared neatly placed like an offering on her pillow, she thought Maman somehow managed the ladder. Later that same evening, as she awoke to a patterned scrabbling on the wall, she suspected a benefactor.

For hasty service, she supposed, or moving from cabin to cabin unnoticed, the upper bunk featured a sliding wall just large enough for a boy, or girl who craves movement, to slip through. If she were mouse-like, Renae could evade the insipid odors of the cabin and perhaps stroll unaccosted on deck.

She was quick-witted enough not to attempt the passage in the middle of the night when ears are tuned for the alarm of an unnatural noise. Her better chance at a little exploration would be in the morning as the adjoining cabin, which she determined must belong to the captain, would most likely be devoid of its occupant. As long as her mother remained bilious, it would be relatively simple to move into the next room without notice.

'Twas adventurous, truly. Renae's toy ship with its deadly whisperings paled by comparison. Here, she had a life-size passage in which to squirrel new secrets. Playing nursemaid was hardly entertaining; and as each wave took them farther from the reach of laws seeking retribution, the memory of her father's demise seemed more game than danger, as if the sea itself absolved her of what she hardly deemed a grievous sin. She regretted it not; therefore, she saw no need to beg forgiveness.

Surely, she reasoned, a man of the sea would harbor secrets that she could turn to advantage. It was a lengthy voyage and she craved diversion. He began the game by gifting her with a book to while away the slowly passing hours. He guessed correctly in assuming she could read, but she knew not why she piqued his curiosity.

When she failed to reveal the source of her volume, she signaled her skill and willingness to engage in subterfuge. Captain Bonneval almost blushed when she met his eyes in recognition at table. He clearly suspected the little family was more than appearances forbore, but he could not fathom the diversion he would provide her as they sailed to the islands.

Her first task was to silence the panel as she slid it open enough to shimmy through. That was solved easily enough with a generous sprinkling of the powder Maman insisted kept lice from taking up residence in her long hair. It would be difficult to fend off the vermin on the bark, especially since Renae saw them speckling the linens on which Maman lay. Of course, in her delirium, Maman mistook the noise of the panel as that of a ship's rat, so perhaps Renae used more caution than necessary, but that only sweetened her game.

The first day, she dared only slip her head into the adjoining bunk. The captain used it as a storage locker. Dear dry goods rose neatly to the ceiling on either side of the bunk: bolts of silk, crates of ladies' shoes, gentlemen's port, and an open basket of oranges threatening to spill out were she not careful. All the goods were hidden behind a curtain identical to the one that offered the only privacy she could have on such a journey. She smiled at the discovery of her hidey-hole and recognized it as a clear invitation from the captain. Why else would he make the path so plain? She had a friend—even better, a conspirator.

Spending most of her life under lock and key made Renae most eager for any expansion of space, even if the price were deceiving her mother. Besides, had Maman not deceived her by failing to reveal the true identity of the cruel lord? Maman was due a turnabout, and a deception undiscovered is no deceit at all. Renae trusted she was clever enough to enjoy a bit of sport. Maman would be none the wiser.

With such a basket of oranges, Captain Bonneval would also be none the wiser if she took just one. If he gave her a passageway, he meant for her to explore. What good was exploration if one can't enjoy the spoils of the discovery? Her hand was around an orange before she completed the thought, her nails already digging into the pithy flesh. Renae peeled the fruit slowly, savoring the sweet tartness on her tongue segment by segment. The juice and thievery energized her, but another round of her mother's endless retching brought her in check. She plunged her fingers deeply in a silken bolt to cut the stickiness and called out, "Coming, Maman. I am here."

The peel, she hastily stuffed into her pillow, for orange essence was a far more pleasant aroma than shit and vomit. Perhaps Maman would die. Perhaps she would recover. Either way, Renae's days of dumping brimming chamber pots out the porthole would soon be relieved. She crossed herself against the sudden wickedness of imagining her own mother dead, but she could endure it. She'd struck the deathblow of her father. Granted, she knew him not at the time, but that was no matter— her mettle was proven. She had no regrets and the compunction to strike again when the need might arise. Yes, she could endure.

"*Merci*, child," Maman rasped as Renae dabbed the cracked corners of her mouth. "Your hands smell of heaven."

"Why, Maman, whatever do you mean? Your sickness has you unawares."

18

Randall

The days at sea dragged on, inching toward sunset after sunset in a maddening ebb and flow of routine. Mornings consisted of a brief, escorted visit to the rail. M. Clemence deftly shielded Cecille and Renae from the harsher realities of life at sea. Certainly, they had no idea of the squalor in the hold or the vile habits of the sailors who added their own water and seed to the depths surrounding them. He kept them tightly cloistered for fear of discovery, which at this point, they stood little chance.

They'd escaped indeed; Cecille just did not realize it yet. That was all the better, for he intended to gentle her, to make her his wife in the truest sense of the word. He knew she intended to part ways as soon as their safety was ensured. He wanted her to need him. The world, whether it be new or old, was an inhospitable place for a woman alone. It simply would not allow for independence. She needed him; she must realize.

She had been caged so long, however, that independence was what she sought most. It was a castle of air, as insubstantial as her ambition to claim *L'Arbol* for her daughter. Perhaps Lord Clemenceau's roughshod handling of such a prize had addled her mind. Any caged creature weakens over time. The woman was headstrong, as was the budding girl, but he'd gentled many an obstinate courser. A woman would be no different.

The greensickness, horrible as it was, blessed them. Cecille accepted his arm and their chaste bunk as naturally as if they were actually husband and wife. The sickness they shared created a facsimile of the silent bond of lovers. He fervently wished to consummate that bond, but like any good horseman, he exerted his will incrementally. The girl served them well during his illness, and he counted it another blessing she was so hale.

She was the very likeness of her mother, excepting her eyes. The girl's eyes would be their undoing were they not half a sea away from *L'Arbol*. He counted on any lords concerned by the unlikelihood of Clemenceau to succumb to a burning bed to be too busy re-parceling his lands to bother themselves with scrutiny. Multiple men benefited from the demise of the lord bastard; so be it.

The steady hand of the girl was the sticking point. Her father's cold eyes peered from her face, searching people as if she were reading them like a printed page, but she would be a beauty like her mother. Renae's "Papa" was so natural, though, so convincing, that it unsettled him. Mayhap he was guilty of reading now. Time and distance, he was certain, would soften the steel of her gaze.

Mother and daughter, he'd come to believe, were not as much mirrored images as opposing sides of a coin. Their mornings at the rail exhibited the greatest contrast. Cecille had not fully recovered from greening and still felt ill, but clearly relished any opportunity to soak in the sun's warmth. By midday, when they took their main meal at table with Bonneval and his Jewish money counter, her pallor improved markedly.

Renae, on the other hand, seemed preoccupied and eager to return to her book below deck. He was unsure how long it should take a young lady to read a volume and pondered how she could occupy her time when the story closed. He had yet to see her work a sampler as was customary for girls her age; Bonneval gave him a sleeve of woven cloth, needle, and thread to occupy the girl, but it remained untouched.

She obeyed and served her mother well, but something was not quite at rights. She seemed to enjoy sitting in her bunk, curtain drawn, separate from the world. The novelty of caring for a kitten, which the girl oddly called Bourrasque, wore thin quickly with the animal's plaintive yowls. A more practical man would have drowned the wretched beast weeks ago, but he did not wish to risk displeasing the girl, or by proxy, her mother. If Captain Bonneval continued his geniality, Randall might convince Renae to make a gift of Bourrasque—every bark needed a rat-catcher aboard.

When she descended from her bunk to sit at the little desk below or tend her mother, the girl looked refreshed. In the height of his fever he would have sworn the pleasing aroma of citrus emanated from her caring hands. Thankfully, she'd taken to tucking her bedraggled hair into a ship's boy's cap she found in her cupboard, as she liked to call her lofted bunk. The cap was as unbecoming as her hair that stood in a mixture of unruly tufts and stringy lengths. When it grew to match her mother's, the locks would complete the illusion of one being of two ages, silver-tipped and iridescent like a sheath of water falling gently off a precipice.

He watched as the last of the day's light illuminated Cecille's flowing hair. She used a narrow comb to work powder through her hair, stopping to tap the ivory teeth at the porthole. She continued to work the comb, flicking away what vermin she could with the merest hint of disdain. It was the most erotic act he'd seen in a woman; private, yet natural as a horse swatting flies with its tail. He knew he would not be able to curtail his desire much longer.

"Shall I read to you, Papa?" Renae asked with that tenor of innocence belied by the discordant emptiness of her calculating eyes. So, she deduced he was no man of letters. All the volumes in the world would be useless to her without a man's protection. Her fondness for books would have to be truncated when they reached home, but for the present, it was helpful, as it kept her out of sight and mischief.

"Renae, why don't you take the lantern to your cupboard and read to yourself? Have a care not to set your curtain ablaze. All the pitch on this bark would set the ship off like a tinder box," he suggested. Bourrasque whined piteously from his wickered cage. "Take your kitten up, too. See if you can get it to cease making that infernal noise."

"Oui, Renae, be a good little mother and settle little Bourrasque," added Cecille as she shooed Renae toward the ladder with her fine bone comb, one of the few items of value Randall had not sold to purchase their safekeeping.

The girl, obedient as ever, unlatched the wicker door and reached into the cage to retrieve the mewling cat. Bourrasque hissed, slashed a quick paw across Renae's outstretched hand, claws out and drawing blood. The sight of four seeping track marks made her eyes narrow, and she shot her hand back in the cage, grabbed the kitten cruelly by the scruff of its neck, and pitched it through the porthole.

"Renny, *non!*" shouted Cecille. Randall pushed the girl aside to peer uselessly into the inky blackness that swallowed the hapless animal. He rounded, grabbing Renae's arm hard and raising his left hand to deliver a well-deserved blow. The girl did not crumble or burst into tears, but shook away the stinging slap and met him with a glare of ice.

"The cat displeased me; it displeased us all. What of it? 'Twas naught but a cat. I've done worse."

"We do not kill for convenience's sake," Randall seethed.

"No, Papa?" she answered with a sneer. "Have you discussed this with Maman?"

"The kitten was an innocent, child," added Cecille.

"The kitten was a nuisance, mother," retorted Renae. "You'd do well to remember yourself, Maman. In your shock, you cried out my old name. I am she no more."

Renae turned to Randall. "And you, sir, shall never strike me again. 'Twould be rather a nuisance, think you not?"

She took the lantern, picked up the volume which had fallen to the floor in the fracas, and ascended the ladder. When she reached the height that allowed her to cast her eyes downward upon two shocked expressions, she smiled sweetly and said, "Goodnight, Maman. Goodnight, Papa," blowing them each a kiss and drawing her curtain as if nothing had happened at all.

19

Renae

After such a show of strength, lying down was impossible. Renae, heady with excitement, decided to celebrate her victory by pilfering another juicy orange from the captain's store. The lantern cast shadows on the wall as she changed into her sleeping shift. The nights were almost balmy lately…; she imagined Bourrasque paddling through the swells, watching the bark sail away in the darkness. The damnable cat had reason to cry now, but mercifully, those cries would go unheard. They may call a creature of the deep to rise up and swallow Bourrasque, carrying him to the mysteries beneath. She should have fed the wretch to the fishes weeks ago.

Her silhouette fell on the sliding wall through which she would soundlessly slip in a few moments. In profile, she could just make out the outline of her budding breasts, and she watched herself explore them with tentative fingers. They were hard little knots for now, but soon would fill out as supple as oranges. She removed her pantalets so the balmy air would caress her through the night. The lantern illuminated a wispy plume of woman's hair peppering the alabaster cleft of her most secret self. Maman instructed her to report when her woman's hair appeared, for it would serve as the harbinger for the monthly courses that would swiftly follow. Renae fished the toy ship from her apron pocket, sprang the trap, and whispered, "I am near woman," into its hold. Satisfied, she tucked her hair back into the ship's boy's cap and prepared to crawl through her mouse hole to the adjoining cabin.

So confident was Renae in her stealth that Captain Bonneval's lamp did not deter her. She crept to the basket of oranges and reached for the largest fruit. Just as she brought the orb to her nose to breathe in its citric essence, the curtain parted and Bonneval's quick hand closed around her wrist. She gasped, caught. With his other hand, he pressed his finger to his lips, then coaxed her to the ladder.

"I see I've found my little mouse," he chuckled softly. "Do not fear. Come sit with me awhile." He shifted his grip from one of entrapment to that of a gentleman leading a lady. She glanced back toward her own cabin and allowed him to help her down the ladder, bare-footed and bare-assed beneath her chemise. She hoped he wouldn't notice, but he was, after all, a ship's captain. He could be trusted.

Bonneval took the orange from her when she was comfortably situated. He sectioned it effortlessly with a pearled knife, placing the segments on a piece of china whose pattern was more exotic than the fruit. The flesh of the orange was more the color of crimson than the sun, its nodules larger than normal and threatening to burst from the profusion of juice it held inside.

"Stealing is a hanging offense in the new world same as the old, little mouse," Bonneval said equably.

She ignored this warning, mesmerized by the sanguine flesh made bare. "What is it?" Renae whispered.

"Why, it is called a blood orange. The old stories say those who share its juices become bound as if by blood."

"Oh, really?" she giggled. "I have little intention of being bound by anything, but I'm curious as to the taste." He speared a segment with his knife and offered it to the girl. Juice trickled down his finger, and he resisted the urge to lick it off. It would not serve to frighten the little thief. She looked rather ridiculous in that cap, but it accented the fullness of her cheeks. He expected that fullness would be echoed as she blossomed and clicked his teeth at the idea of running his hands along her rounded bottom.

"Shall I have you arrested when we land?"

She took another slice of orange, completely nonplussed by his threat. "What would be the sport in that, pray?" Renae traced her lips with the fruit the way she had spied Maman do in gentler couplings back in France. The blood orange stained her lips an alluring crimson that made the captain want to take her right there, though she was likely not yet a woman. Did the girl even realize what she was doing? He clicked his teeth again and shifted his glance. His eye settled on the meager bookshelf he kept beside his feathered bunk.

"Have you finished your volume, Mademoiselle?"

"I've read it thrice," she replied. "Have you another?"

"I have many, but it grows late, and we must not have you found amiss." He ushered her back to the ladder. "Return tomorrow evening, and I shall select one for you. I have much to show you, little mouse."

"I trust we must keep these meetings furtive?" she asked with an intoxicating mixture of innocence and mischief.

"*D'accord*. We shall be bosom friends. Would you like that?"

"'Twould certainly relieve this *ennui*," she replied.

"Then we shall be strange at noon meal and intimates in secrecy. Here, give me your hand." He gently kissed each finger then sent her on her way. "*Bonsoir*, my little mouse."

"*Bonsoir*, my captain." The moniker sounded delicious rolling off her tongue.

20

Cecille

The unholy union with Randall must be consummated immediately, for Cecille finally accepted what should have been obvious—she carried a child. Only a most vengeful God would rain down such wrath against her, would make her feel the irony of taking a life whilst another was begat. There were cures, purgatives, and wise woman's tales that would rid her of his seed, but nonesuch were available on this bark, *The Praying Mantis*. What a cruel twist of fate to grant the bastard power beyond the grave. Unless some happy accident befell her, no number of petticoats or aprons could conceal her condition by the time she set foot on dry land.

The only viable solution was to have Clemence and have him immediately. All his boasts of lessons as recompense for his assistance proved impotent. He recovered a fortnight ago from the greensickness which continued to vex her in the mornings—how could she misread this sign—and had yet to take her despite lying with her nightly.

It was time to take matters into her own hands. The girl's insolence proved she also failed to cool the father's blood coursing through her veins. Had the girl been born a son, their futures would have looked quite different. That was not to be. Renae would have been better served sucking the poison from the sweetmeats she helped prepare for her father. She was a bit young, but of a marriageable age. Cecille would have done with her expediently.

But this babe inside, a boy certainly as that would complete God's wrath, could still outreach her so long as he has a father. Randall would do, must do. He was kind to her and the girl. He felt a sense of duty, of responsibility on which she would fix her hopes. He would be easy to dupe, as all men are with the intricacies of birth. Yes, she must act this very night.

***

Renae slipped through the aperture and passed silently into Bonneval's chamber. He presented some new curiosity to share with her each evening. He spoke in deep, soothing tones that melted like marzipan in her ears, and his caresses plied her muscles, both relaxing her and sending odd tickling sensations deep within. They were being wicked, she knew, but that made their game all the more entertaining. They were too clever to be found out. She wondered what Bonneval would do when they reached the Antilles. Would he ask for her hand? Had he a wife, old and fat, waiting for him with nothing more to offer than hot mutton pie? She could defeat her with a smile.

He was old; a man of thirty-five, he told her. He was a great, cunning sea captain, he told her, and he wished to keep her as a pet for her to blossom like a fine peony under his tutelage. After she blossomed, though, and they made landfall, she would be a pet no more. His hand explored the region of her thigh from under the table as if it were a thing separate from him, from their conversation. The fingers inched upward, ever upward, but she shied, standing from the table to gain some space to breathe. His caresses brought on a quickening deep within her belly that was difficult to identify. She was shy and bold at once. She wanted his hand to find the mark, but did not trust how her body might react when he reached it.

***

113

Cecille lay back to back with Randall as had become their custom on the voyage. She slowly unbuttoned her nightdress, taking care not to startle Randall, whose modulated breathing suggested that nether land between wakefulness and sleep. She positioned the muslin to fall open when she shifted. Her hand brushed the curve of her belly, already beginning to round. She turned, pressed herself against him and whispered his name. He turned immediately to her, taking her in his arms. "I've been waiting for you to call my name," he said gruffly as his hands flew in his haste.

***

"You are radiant, my little mouse," he said almost gruffly and clicked his teeth within his mouth. "Don't retreat. Would you like to see the secret part of a man?"

"Do you mean the fucking part, Captain?" She spied and heard enough of her mother's use to recognize a man's cock stretching against his trousers. Coupling must be painful judging by her mother's outcries, but she was curious nonetheless.

"What a word from such an innocent! Wherever could you have learnt that? No, not for fucking; you have yet to bloom. I would not spoil the prize ere it is ripe for the fucking."

"We shall reach our destination before that, so you shall never have your fuck," Renae responded matter-of-factly.

"Oh, I wager you shall look for the *Mantis* and your captain every day. I am nothing, if not a man of patience. The days will be long and hot; you'll long for the sea breeze and the gentle sway of the *Mantis* upon the swells."

"This talk makes me feel odd. I'm going to bed." She scurried up the ladder as Captain Bonneval chuckled, clicking his teeth like a beast nipping at her heels.

***

114

He was a curious man; hasty yet gentle; hungry, even ravenous, yet sure; hell-bent, yet accommodating. He did not become lost in his own lust, reducing her to a mere vessel into which he spent himself. He reined his desire, an intoxicating mixture of power without force, persistence without presumption. This man did not take her, rutting like a carnal beast in a display of dominance, but curried her favor in such a manner that she found herself rising to meet his thrusts. He was a most curious man.

Cecille thought of the growing babe as Randall snored contentedly, an arm tossed assuredly across her stomach. She thought of his seed within and the odd, burning sensation that accompanied the coupling. He was no gentleman, but he redeemed her from an intolerable existence. He could not restore her to the power of her position as lady, albeit mistress if she laid truth bare, of *L'Arbol*. He vouchsafed the passage for them all, protecting them from the ills, real or imagined, she was not completely certain, of the long months at sea.

He showed nothing but kindness, even when disciplining Renae. Her act of cruelty toward the squalling cat followed by her insolence would not be forgotten. The child's haughtiness was of Cecille's own design, built on empty dreams of privilege, neglect, and nursed by a desire for vengeance. She created Renae's shortcomings out of her own ambition. Although she harbored a modicum of regret, the real blame she left spitted and roasting in a bed that she prayed was but a precursor of the hellfires he surely suffered.

Whether by blood or nurture, Renae was a facsimile of her father—unapologetically cruel. Her key role in their quest for freedom quickened a proclivity that would lie dormant no more. Renae would wield her power eventually; of this, Cecille was sure. The incident with the poor kitten was a mere sampling of a girl convinced she acts with impunity. She would have her comeuppance, Cecille doubted not.

Renae was spoiled, soiled by witnessing her mother's degradation and participating in a murder, however well-deserved. She harbored indignation with an unnatural savoring. The girl hungered for vengeance and was willing to bide her time. Cecille would continue to placate her for the present, but any maternal sense of love, pride, or preservation disappeared as suddenly and irrevocably as that cat through the porthole.

The child was a bad seed…, intelligent, cunning even, but with a penchant for cruelty. She must be married off before she mars the baby with her vindictive spirit. Cecille would see to making arrangements as soon as they made landfall. Renae had yet to reach her potential, and though she felt a sliver of compunction for the poor bastard whose head Renae should one day turn, she still had enough personal ambition to attempt a suitable match.

The burning deep inside her loins continued beyond the coupling with Randall, which was now a nightly expectation. Whether from the nipping fleas and lice infesting their bedclothes and their very persons, no matter how frequently she plucked the vermin with her comb, or from her blessed state, Cecille vacillated between a vague physical discomfort and an odd sort of numbness. Her womb sometimes felt as if it were falling asleep, much as the sensation an arm may have if one leans against the rail too long.

Her condition would be obvious soon enough, but the ultimate deception would be simple so long as the child resembled her. Even if he bore the visage of Clemenceau, she would have Randall well in hand by that time. Oftentimes, babies did not show their true semblance for well over a year. Bald and mewling, one infant looks much like another. Cecille had time on her side now, and she intended to see her way through this course.

Besides, she was beginning to enjoy Randall's attentions. It was pleasing to be caressed rather than handled. She envisioned herself enjoying his company for a very long time. The child bound her to him, of course, but it also liberated her. It was an apt time for God to smile upon her path.

She pressed her hands along the changing contours of her stomach in the age-old gesture of maternal instinct, anticipating the first fluttered bubbling within that signified a quickening of life. She longed for a looking glass so she could examine the changes, but it would be weeks before she would have that luxury. Surely, the Antilles were not so rude as to be devoid of such simple niceties.

Cecille glanced about the cramped cabin and sighed. She could never endure a life at sea. Why, it bore quite a semblance to life in a locked room above a tavern. This time, instead of iron bolts, the unchanging horizon hemmed her in place.

What woman was without bonds? What woman did not create bond upon bond, locking herself safely within layered handfasts of marriage, of motherhood, of vocation, of circumstance? The cage may be oaken like this vessel carrying them from one world into another. The cage may be a damasked sitting room softened by the warmth of a roaring grate, but it was a cage nonetheless. Whatever bounds she escaped, she used their loose ends to knot new ones afresh.

Life must be a series of entanglements, its struggle to relieve the pressure on bindings that choke and to stretch the tethers of whatever affords a sensation of freedom, however brief. For freedom is but illusion. Men chase it, risk their livelihoods for it, die for it. For women, freedom is an impossibility—society demands a blood price for protection of the weaker sex.

But Maisie Sessile had tasted freedom: heady, warm, salty. For one brief moment, she'd held the power as she watched the awful recognition dawn in his eyes at the precise instant their light dimmed forever.

Then, it slipped like water through her fingers and Maisie Sessile was no more, as dead as the man whose bed had ignited in flames she'd devoutly wished were a Hell-greeting for his immortal soul. Her former self reduced to ashes, she reached for a new name, a new place, a new life. Galloping away in the night, she knitted new bonds, locking herself, her daughter, and this man who offered love into another sort of cage, but a cage nonetheless.

Freedom, perhaps, is not meant to be sought, but found within the confines of the cages we build for ourselves. Mayhap that is why men like Captain Bonneval thrive at sea, bobbing like a cork in the vast ever-ness of the depths. His purser, Jew no matter, relished the confined rows of infinite figures. And Randall Clemence, husband in practicality and practice, would secure their handfast by accepting the child she carried as his own, not because of her deception, but because of his own willingness to be deceived.

This, Cecille recognized, was the heart of the chasm that continued to expand between her and her daughter. Renae also got a taste of freedom. She overestimated her power to press her will; she miscalculated the breadth of headstrong independence, assuming her mother's steadfast support as she plumbed the depth of her resolve. Renae thought her weak for leaning on the support of Randall Clemence, for taking her place as helpmeet in this game of chance. She simply traded one cage for another. But 'twas untrue. Randall would be the bedrock on which she built a new existence. Her son would have a name, something Renae could never claim.

Renae knew seclusion, but she had yet to experience loneliness. Her sequester from the greater world created a false sense of self; the child was her own idol. She seemed to thrive in the close quarters of the *Mantis*, smelling of blossoms as she herself transformed. Cecille thought the shift a bit early, but Renae was a prescient child in every other aspect, so it stood to reason she would mature quickly. That, of course, would allow Cecille to move all the more rapidly to find a match for her and have her away before she could interfere.

Her quick rages could be tempered with a firm hand, but her absolute lack of remorse coupled with the haughty disdain in her

118

eyes was unnerving. Cecille could not act until landfall, though. There was much to be done in establishing lodging and acclimating to a new world where, according to Captain Bonneval, none were too interested in the past. Her lying-in time would be the perfect opportunity to move Renae toward marriage, preferably to a man on another isle.

21

Bonneval

Something about the girl's eyes was arresting. Yes, they changed hue in the nuances of light or mood, but it was deeper than that. Some clandestine knowledge gave her unbridled confidence. Some darkness pooled beneath the surface, like the shadow of a whale matching speed alongside the *Mantis*, invisible to the untrained eye.

He found that darkness enticing—not to ferret out and expose to the light—that would be as dull and common as the brace of whores having their run through the crew. He always provided a ready fuck or two on the crossings to keep his men refreshed. Naturally, he tested their seaworthiness before setting the Jew upon them to broker their passage. On occasion, he'd bring a ship's boy aboard for additional sport. When the girl donned the hat left in her berth, she was positively arousing.

His appetite, however, did not extend to children, as delicious as that darkness of her glance appeared. His teeth clicked together as he imagined her whispering her truth against his throat, sliding her tongue in flicking tendrils about the hairs on his chest and teasing his nipples with her chin as her hand explored beneath his breeches. Oh, she was on the very cusp of ripening. He would know all. His wait, an ecstatic agony, would not be long.

The girl came to him nightly now, shimmying deftly down the ladder to drink in whatever treat or bauble he had to offer. She adored blood oranges, of which he was in low supply, and the books he quite innocently brought to noon meal with her parents, whose newfound infatuation with one another served to confirm his suspicion they were not what they claimed to be. The sea has a way of making its own truths, though, so he cared not a whit for their weak-watered deception.

She took to inserting bawdy notes for him in the margins of the volumes she returned and thrilled to handing them over to him under her mother's very nose. The mixture of innocence and experience, innuendo and gullibility, was as intoxicating as it was heady. He would most certainly enjoy tupping this one. If she proved the catch he thought she might, he might even marry her. She joked about his wife, old and fat, waiting for him back home in France. He did not correct her, but she would be quite surprised to find his wife in prime condition on La Desirade. That is, if he had any intention of introducing them.

Renae was hardly the first daughter deflowered by sweetings from the captain. The tight quarters and inherent dangers of the sea made legs part as readily as waves at the bow-head. She was, however, the most intriguing. He would check with Ephraim to see if the coffers could support another quayside cottage, perhaps in the Port of New Orleans or Port of Mobile. He had yet to create a suitable diversion for those legs of his travels. He surmised the child might whet his appetite for quite some time, as young as she was.

He was quite a dutiful husband in port, really, the very likeness of domesticity. Neither of his wives had the slightest inkling of the other's existence across the ocean. Thus far, he had only produced three puling girls, making his game all the more simplistic as he had no son to tag along after his father on future voyages. Bonneval grinned at his own fortune. It was quite the happy arrangement.

She allowed him to stroke her hair now. The fine boar bristles tamed her locks at least for a while until they started to crackle like lightning tracing a grey sky. Then random hairs would stand on end, silveresque filaments, and she would clamp the boy's hat over her ears to rein in the wildness. She laughed aloud at the thought of a perfectly bald man owning such a brush, but he spoke in soothing tones as he stroked her, painting word pictures of the islands and the adventures of the Americas beyond.

He traced gentle kisses on the back of her neck, so fluttering and embedded in story she seemed not to notice. The brush followed the path of her neck down to her shoulders and she submitted to the strokes much like a cat pleasuring in a good scratch.

"Here, Benne," she said, "Allow me." She took the brush in hand, rose, and sat him down in her place. Giggling, she ran the bristles over his slick head. She leaned in closely as she observed the tiny red trails the brush forged on his skin. He fingered her shimmy as she worked, plying the fabric between his fingers in rhythm with the circling strokes of the brush. Mimicking him, she drew her lips to his ear and spoke in a throaty whisper.

"Benne, take me there; take me to Alabama."

Her lips brushed his lobe as she pronounced the exotic word, a thousand times more erotic than the tingling of his scalp. He spun her onto his lap, and this time she didn't shy away.

"What of your mother?"

"She daren't stand in our way."

"And your father?" She turned her head sideways as she thought and then laughed triumphantly.

"I can assure you, my father will speak not a word."

"And your guardian?" Her eyes widened, and she stood, planting a kiss coquettishly on his forehead. Her smile held even while her tone dropped.

"You are quite clever, Benne. I expect he will keep silence just as you."

"What if it profits him to speak, my mouse?"

"Then he shall be silenced."

Climbing up the ladder, she turned and fixed the captain with a glare that was icy and impassioned all at once. Her eyes darkened in a quick rage she held well in check. He steadied himself and when she was sure she had his complete attention, she traced her lower lip with her finger seductively and clicked her teeth. He was hers.

22

Cecille

They started out as thin lines on the westward horizon, sketched low in the sky, almost like scurrying clouds or bursts of surf escaping their watery bounds. Their squawks carried across the water and were punctuated by the rhythmic concussions of the *Mantis* cutting the waves and the animation in the shouts of the crew.

"Shorebirds," stated Randall at her elbow. "The islands are at hand." They stood together watching the patterns traced by the distant flocks.

"I do not wish to part from you," he whispered.

"Nor I you," Cecille returned as she rested her head on his shoulder. The baby rolled at that very moment, whether in approval or protest she did not know. But the movement was quickly followed by a burning so intense, she shifted position uncomfortably.

"Is it the child?"

"Aye. Nay. I am unsure. You know?"

"Yes, Cecille, I know. I know more than you allow." Randall turned her to face him. "We have escaped, Cecille. No one shall seek retribution across the sea. I shan't permit the child to be fatherless." He paused to ascertain she understood his meaning. "We have been blessed, rarely blessed, with the opportunity to begin anew."

Taking both her hands in his, Randall knelt, pressing his forehead to her waist. "Be he of my loins or of the past, he shall be born in a new world. I lay claim to this child and the mother who carries him."

Cecille extracted her hand to wipe away the tears from her eyes. God blessed her at last. She helped Him along the way, of course, but the relief of gaining a name, if not a fortune, for the child would be enough. She need scrabble no more for a place, for a sense of self, for a purpose beyond chattel. Whore no longer, Cecille now fulfilled the role of wife. This child indeed heralded a second chance. She would send Renae packing toward a life to forge on her own and cleave from the past forevermore.

The salt air carried on it the kiss of summer and the fragrance of blooms she would soon set to vase as she imagined her island home. Servants would be aplenty, and her experience managing the household of *L'Arbol* would serve her well in this new environ. She relished the thought of a cleansing soak in the copper tub Captain Bonneval and the Jewish purser readied for their privileged passengers. Many a louse would meet its doom in that tub within a greater tub of a ship, and she would be rid of the vermin dogging her clear across the ocean.

The purser rearranged rigging and extra canvas to create privacy for the bathers on deck. Only a sailor aloft in the crow's nest would be able to peer at the tub whose occupant naturally gazed beyond the dipping bow as they steeped in the heated water like pasty tea bags. The men already cast their lots for climbing duty, and Bonneval chose his time wisely for personally inspecting the moonraker, the topmost sail designed to give the *Mantis* extra speed and agility.

His curiosity as to the condition of Cecille Clemence outpaced his pent-up desire for the girl. She would be had soon enough. He suspected Mm. Clemence to be a bit farther along with child than decency forbears. He did not need a Jew counter to make those simple calculations. Surely, her foray across the sea did not hinge solely on the undesired result of indiscretion. Purgatives and midwives were readily available solutions for such dalliance.

125

As she undoubtedly turned her affections toward Randall Clemence, whose identity was dubious, the child she carries may prove either deuce or trump in her scheme, whatever it may be. The two were besotted, forsooth, making stolen moments with the comely daughter hardly sporting. The blush of newfound lust coupled with the luscious fullness pregnancy brings to a woman's dugs would create a fetching spectacle. He decided to give the girl first bidding, but 'twas for her mother he would scale the rigs.

Cecille recognized the glint of victorious superiority in Renae's eye when the girl announced she held the initial appointment with the copper slipper, as she called it. The girl was scheming; so recognizable it was almost like looking into a mirror of her younger self all those years ago, stealing away to the granary to take hold of Lord Clemenceau's cock and what she thought to be destiny.

Caught up in the setting of her own snares, Renae assumed her ploys went unnoticed. Cecille checked the raising of her eyebrows at the announcement and quickly nodded her assent. The girl would have the virgin bath, with the water at its ripeness of purity and temperature. How fitting. Cecille would take advantage of this opportunity to discover the girl's designs.

Renae, escorted of course by Randall, had yet the time to reach the deck before Cecille ascended the ladder and peered into the dim berth. Unable to detect anything unusual, she descended quickly to fetch the lantern. She returned to find an over-ripened orange hidden beneath the pillow. She pierced its flesh with a pearl-inlaid paring knife she found lying beside it, splitting the fruit with surprising ease, for the knife was honed sharp. It oozed crimson juice as delicious as it was alarming. Cecille munched the fruit greedily as she inspected. Only the captain would have access to such a delicacy. The thought of his name barely registered in her mind when she saw it: a discreet panel in the wall. She placed the orange peelings under Renee's pillow to blaze her discovery and in moments slid open what she suspected to be a hidden compartment.

126

Cecille's size prevented her from squeezing through the opening, but clearly this was much more than a niche for holding childish novelties. 'Twas a passageway into the captain's quarters! So, this is the explanation for those closeted hours of reading. She was toying with the captain, or he with her. The austere debaucher was likely spying on her at this moment. Cecille said a quick prayer that the girl's virginity remained intact, but no matter, really. Eager bridegrooms are easily duped.

Satisfied and somewhat proud of the girl's ability to wrest treats from the parsimonious captain, Cecille closed the panel and returned to her part of the cabin. She glanced at the filthy bedding. She was not sure how much good a bath would actually do when the linens were not refreshed, but passing up the pleasure of a warm-water soak would be folly. She stood at the porthole and turned her attention to her growing son. Naturally, he would be named for his father.

Randall returned momentarily to escort Cecille to the copper slipper. "Where is Renae?" she asked immediately.

"I left her at the rail on the kind arm of the Captain. He states he has some pressing business aloft and bid me to hand you readily to the purser," Randall replied.

"*D'accord.* We wouldn't want to keep the Captain waiting." Cecille rose at once. "Do you think Bonneval fancies Renae?"

"Because he favored her with the first bath? No, he's just being kindly. Why, he is old enough to be her father," Randall laughed. "I've half a mind to hop into that copper slipper with you, my beauty."

"Scandalous!" she replied, giggling. "Don't give the purser any ideas. He would gladly charge the accounts double for the same bath." They laughed heartily as they made their way on deck.

23

Bonneval

Grimacing as he climbed, Bonneval chuckled at the thought of exacerbating the knee he twisted months ago when he slipped on the deck. He masked the injury well, but the joint now served as an accurate predictor of squalls. It was worth a bit of swelling to satisfy his curiosity about the swelling of Mm. Cecille's midsection, which would be on full display if not for Ephraim's unfortunate decision to provide Mme. Renae with bubbling soap. The copper slipper was not frothy, but milky in color, so he would simply have to hang about the ropes until Mm. Cecille emerged from her bath.

He was constantly amazed at how generally unobservant people could be. He plainly saw M. Clemence waiting patiently just outside the makeshift room. The man had but to look up slightly to see his shadow cast upon the sailcloth. Even the smallest drop of regard would lead his eyes upward to the captain, who clearly had the ideal vantage point for espying unsuspecting bathers.

Experience and faith told him, however, that the smith—as he purported to be despite a decided dearth of cracked knuckles; the man either swung his hammer to perfection or lied—would fain glance skyward. His eyes were on the isles rising steadily on the horizon. It might be a service to the man to suggest he singe the hairs from his forearms if he wished to continue the ruse ashore. The warm waters of the bath would draw the bather's eyes within, basking in comfort as she soaked. He was perfectly concealed in his perch.

Observation was at the root of his intrigue with the girl. Her allure rested not so much in her physical prescience as in her powers of observation. Renae read people as if she were reading a book, synthesizing tone and gesture to formulate strikingly accurate conclusions. She did this with an utter lack of compunction. Her age and experience, which he was teasing from her caress by caress, lent her a façade of invincibility. His age and experience lent him recognition of the façade. Of course, he could read people as well, and this in itself made her an appealing conquest.

Cecille shifted uncomfortably in the copper slipper. The water was of a temperature warm enough for her exposed skin to prickle even in the tropic heat of the day, but that was not the problem. The burning sensation in her womb returned. The lye in the soapy water must be irritating her private areas. This was probably why the old midwives advised against bathing while with child. They argued that water entering a woman's cavity could drown the baby, but Cecille thought this to be nonsense. When a woman gave birth, a rush of water, piss, and blood preceded the child's appearance into the world. A baby is quite accustomed to immersion.

Her delicate parts, however, were protesting loudly against the strong soap. Scrubbing with a bit of the cloth lining the tub did nothing but produce a pink tinge and increase her discomfort. She rose from the tub within minutes, much to the satisfaction of the captain.

Later, Cecille squirmed in the bunk, her cleanliness serving mostly to entice the vermin crawling in the ticking. Reversing the linens did little to alleviate her constant itching; the bedding should be dumped in the sea. She lay awake fighting the urge to scratch and disturb Randall's even breathing, and listened.

She almost succumbed to sleep when she heard it: the soft, mousey scraping of the secret door sliding open in Renae's berth above. It was unmistakable now that she knew what to attend to, and she knew she had heard this selfsame sound many nights

129

before, assuming it to be the scrabble of ship's rats. The captain was keeping company with her daughter, of this she was now certain.

Renae had quite forgotten the blood orange under her pillow, especially since its telltale lump was not evident when she entered her bunk. She sat waiting for the sleep sounds from below, almost too excited to keep from wiggling like a child. It happened at last, right in the copper slipper. As she bathed, she felt an odd warming sensation that could only be the quickening of her womanhood. The coin-sized spot of crimson on the pantalettes she held in her hand was the proof and 'twas worth far more than mere passage. The captain would surely take her now and in that union, take her as his wife on to the Port of New Orleans or perhaps even the Port of Mobile. These place names rolled exotically off her tongue as she imagined herself a captain's wife.

She would be free to do as she pleased, for she would be out of the eye of her mother and he would be at sea most of the year. Kept but not checked, her status would afford myriad opportunities to toy as she might. He was old and quite bald. The captain would surely die before her charms faded. Renae furrowed her brow. She needed him long enough to make her way and secure his fortune, which must be vast considering the quality of the items he kept ferreted away in his cabin.

Beyond that, she cared not and was confident enough to trust herself to find a suitable way to cross that river when she arrived at its banks. She remembered the silken gowns and tufted nursery of her childhood before Maman spoilt their fortune with her stupidity. She may not rise to that level of opulence again, but rise she would.

Renae descended into the captain's quarters swiftly and found him stripped to the waist. Before he turned, she noted that unlike his head, his bare back was peppered with black hairs. It was muscular, though, and tanned from years of sailing, she supposed.

130

"How now, my mouse," Bonneval smiled, "Have you come for a bit of sport?"

"Indeed," she replied and sat before he bid her, quite as if it were her cabin rather than his. The girl, cocksure in her charms, smiled as if she had a secret barely contained by her droll lips. Her eyes fairly sparkled under that ridiculous hat she insisted on wearing.

"Well, out with it. Are you finally going to tell me you killed that poor cat?"

"That?" she giggled, "'twas naught but a cat. No, Benne, I have the news you've been waiting for." She paused for effect. "I have at last reached my womanhood." She said it so matter-of-factly he dared not laugh. He stepped away from her.

"Are you quite sure?"

She clicked her teeth in reply. Cecille did not hear the door slide back into place until just before dawn.

24

Cecille

Renae discovered the orange peels under her pillow once day broke and knew her mother had inspected her belongings in her absence. What she could not discern was whether or not Maman had discovered the passage into Captain Bonneval's quarters. She dare not confront Maman regarding the eaten orange and privy breach without risking the revelation of a plethora of secrets. She would read Maman's eyes at noon meal and ascertain the extent of her knowledge.

Cecille lay abed later than usual to sort the situation. Appearances were important to Bonneval, so a hasty marriage may be forced. In order for that to occur, though, she and Randall must confront the captain. To call his actions into question could mean calling their own actions into question. It would be most difficult to make a public complaint while remaining out of the public eye, even with an island magistrate who would be, after all, quite French. The sea may not be as wide as Randall presumes.

The girl's coquetry was problematic. Cecille had no definitive proof the girl had been despoiled, but circumstances and her own appetites, which surely must pass down from mother to daughter, bespoke the truth. It was a game of cat and mouse for Renae, who was headstrong enough to cut the very head off the *Mantis* itself if need be, to have her way. Bonneval would have his comeuppance, but she dare not risk it by her hand. She would not speak a word: not to Randall, not to the panderer Bonneval, and most certainly not to Renae.

Her motherly instincts lay solely with the baby, and her sense of self-preservation necessitated that her daughter, already lost, lie in the bed she made for herself. This passage changed her, took away the bile that poisoned her mind. She regretted not her actions in the tavern, but she refused to let herself be defined by them or consumed by the horrors that warranted them. She must build a future with no roots in the past.

Cecille thought of the acorns stored inside the toy ship that represented her voyage to freedom. She wanted them back in her possession, not to plant and form a new *L'Arbol* as she previously intended, but to destroy. She would toss that life into the ocean as nonchalantly as her Renae, precious no more, jettisoned the kitten.

Noon meal, their last aboard the *Mantis*, confirmed the relationship. Only Randall failed to detect the source of the energy in the closeted dining room, so focused was he on the landing scheduled for the morrow. Even the purser's eyes shifted bemusedly from Bonneval to the members of the family as he watched the flickers of passion bleed through in this game of cat and mouse round the table. It was a comedy of manners. The moment of revelation was not defined by a single action, but by a series of tiny non-actions, innuendo of gesture, and a lingering of intent that was almost jarring in its silence.

"You ladies have made my luncheon quite pleasant this voyage," began the captain gallantly, "and I would like to present you these fine parasols in appreciation of all your kind attention." Ephraim rose immediately and produced the gifts, proffering first choice to the daughter, a faux pas even a common miller would fail to make. Cecille chose to ignore the slight, but Renae bristled with pride. She recognized her triumph over her mother, relishing her position of superiority.

"You will want to use them in the morn, not to shield the island sun, but to shield yourselves from the island birds who are both numerous and most curious as the ship berths. They can be quite indelicate," Bonneval indicated.

133

Randall chuckled, "In that case, I shall certainly don my cap."

***

Renae slipped her shift back over her head and sighed, either with satisfaction or boredom. Bonneval was unsure which as he traced feathery kisses from the tip of her earlobe down the cord of her neck, darting his tongue playfully on its course to her clavicle. "We shall have to part, just for a time, while I keep company with my wife."

She pulled away. "Your wife? You said she was in France."

"Aye, that I did," he returned with a click of his teeth. Renae was quick, reasoning out the worst, and regarding him with amusement rather than judgment.

"So, you have a second wife in the islands and you wish for another for your American ventures? Do they know of your arrangements?"

"Of course not. Only you are clever enough to have guessed the truth, my mouse."

Renae giggled girlishly. "What a lovely ruse, Benne! An old hag on either side of the ocean, and a warm, lusty bed waiting in Mobile! Is that how you will have me, as your port whore?"

"If it pleases you. I'll marry you, also, if need be."

She became quite serious.

"Oh, yes, Benne. There need be. If I am to be had, I shall be kept and kept handsomely."

He checked at her surety.

"Mouse, you have been had, but nevertheless I shall keep you. I am a man and can love you or destroy you as I will."

"One does not have to be a man to destroy, Benne."

"You are an uncommon woman, Renny."

It was the first time he called her a woman and the first time her true name crossed his lips, even if only by happenstance. Her ears drank in the sound, both old and new simultaneously. She

134

slipped into her name like a fine leather boot, the kind she once wore and would surely wear again. Buttoned up and comfortable, this new old name felt entirely appropriate for the venture on her horizon. Renny Bonneval would be far from entrapped in the Port of Mobile.

***

They gathered on the deck, parasols aloft, to watch the *Mantis* navigate its way painstakingly toward the quay. Dark-skinned natives and nuns in their habits mingled along the boardwalk as birds flocked overhead, eager to find a scrap on the ship or perhaps enamored with the wingspan of the sails. Slowly, other passengers, passengers Renny quite forgot were aboard the *Mantis* in her sequestered crossing, emerged blinking in the tropic brightness. A pair of gaily dressed women carried parasols similar to hers. The Captain's gifts were far from exclusive. They eyed her with apparent disdain but did not speak.

Colors took on an unaccustomed sharpness. The shallows competed with the sky in a contest of blues. Whitecaps, for the sea was choppy this day, marched toward a silver expanse of beach rimming the island in a band. Beyond that, a green almost vulgar in its lushness rose up to surprising height. Cashews peppered the expanse, blurring the line between sand and the verdant lushness rising to snatch feathery billows from the sky.

The Praying Mantis took on a sharpness of its own. The opening of the hold and the hidden innards of the ship brought out the pungency of months of close living. 'Twas not as pronounced as a slaver, Captain Bonneval told her mother, nor was everyone on board privy to the luxury of a porthole much less a soak in the copper slipper. When sailing with workers or animals in the hold, a certain reek was to be expected. The good captain, ever mindful of the sensitivities of his berthed passengers, presented both Renny and Cecille dainty handkerchiefs.

"Ephraim soaks these in his own orange peel concoction to counteract the odor. You'll find these a pleasant distraction until the sea breeze can cleanse the *Mantis*," stated Bonneval.

"Thank you, Captain, you've been quite kind to our family on this journey," said Cecille, looking directly on her daughter. "I should like to ask your intentions."

Renae held her mother's gaze, eyes widening ever so slightly in surprise at her bluntness, but the captain's furtive glance at her daughter did not go unnoticed. His recovery, however, was swift. "I intend to take on dry goods and sail for the Port of Orleans three days hence," he deflected as the birds screeched overhead, parrying with the sails. "Are you quite well, M. Cecille? You appear pained. We shall be docked within the hour. I am certain a turnabout on land will do you good."

He nodded to Randall, who seemed almost fixated by the island bobbing before them. "I must bid you ladies adieu as I guide her in."

He lifted Cecille's hand for a chaste kiss. She did not miss the quick dart of his tongue or the bizarre clicking of his teeth as he took her daughter's hand.

As more people appeared on deck, and sailors barked orders at one another, *The Praying Mantis* took on an almost jovial atmosphere. The sight of home, albeit new and strange, cheered the passengers. If not for the infernal squawking of the birds and the rather unpleasant result of their congregation in the sails, Cecille could have joined in the revelry.

Thankful as she was for Bonneval's foresight in providing parasols and scented handkerchiefs, she could not forget that the niceties were all priced, precisely columned and recorded by the ever-faithful purser, whose silent usury padded Bonneval's pocket handsomely. Something untoward about their relationship raised a stench almost as detectable as that emanating from the hold, but, since the destination was reached, and their escape was assured, it was really none of her concern.

That the good captain padded his lap with her daughter was likely as much the girl's curiosity as the captain's dalliance. She lay the blame for that seduction at Renae's feet. Time, of course, would heal her of this infatuation, and she should be able to make a sound match within a year. She would deal with her daughter's insolence and appetites later, for a more pressing issue was at hand.

The morning piss bucket was pinked with blood. The burning continued well after she pitched the contents out the porthole into the sea. In addition, she felt bilious and weak, almost like the greensickness was upon her again, andirons marking the endpoints of her crucible by sea. Cecille pushed on her stomach in an attempt to get the babe off of her bladder, pressing against the rail as the cacophony around her rose to a fevered pitch. The noise, the glare, the swirling colors of parasols, and the pounding of the *Mantis* through the breakers made her wonder that she should not be safer down below, but her desire to see the ship moored after interminable weeks of nothing but the sea and sky was greater than her need to rest, at least at this moment.

The babe needed solid ground; that was all. She would begin her lying-in immediately, depending on Randall's devotion to settle the details with the remainder of Lord Clemenceau's purse, which rested secure under his blouson as they prepared to disembark. Yes, she must deal with Mme. Renae as soon after the baby's birth as possible, but she would keep, especially in light of Captain Bonneval's imminent departure. For now, Cecille simply sought relief.

The deck, bespattered with the offal of the swarming gulls above and the occasional ejaculation of sea spray from below became treacherous, especially for those unaccustomed to the hazards of life at sea. Some unfortunate mate with the inglorious task of swabbing the deck made quite the comic scene as birds shat behind him in what appeared a concentrated effort to undo his hard labors. Cecille, however, was quite safe beneath her

137

parasol at the rail. Randall, meanwhile, guided Renae to the seaward side as she expressed a desire to bid farewell to the ocean that had been their crude home these many weeks.

Fortune smiles upon the makers, the ones who take their own destinies in hand and leap into the future. The only certainties in life are the uncertainties, and it is on those very uncertainties that the fortunate depend. It is quite the dance, really. At times, even beautiful in its languor or its heated rush, bodies grinding against one another as they clamber for position. Cecille thought about this truth, the truth of uncertainty, as she imagined her new life as a wife. In the purse remained enough gold to secure a modest home in which to raise her new family in blessed obscurity.

The figures on the quay grew larger as the *Mantis* rose on the swells only to disappear in the troughs as she made her way through the break, and Cecille insinuated herself into their lives, imagining her place as she brought her son dockside to goggle at the ships. She scanned the hillside rising up from the bay and thanked God for making her pathway straight toward this new life, the providence of a good match—and quickly—for Renae, and a safe birth for her son. His answer was a trickle of blood sliding down her inner thigh and a sudden screech whose sharpness silenced the boisterous gulls.

25

Renny

If ever a moment evoked a prayer of thanksgiving, this was it. The shit-slicked deck, the pitch of the ship in the swells, the focus of the passengers' attention at the bow as the *Mantis* made for the calm waters of the bay, and the sailors' busyness found Renny and the ever-present Randall momentarily alone aft. His slip was her opportunity. The unfortunate timing of his fall was her gift from God.

Randall, stupefied by the impact of the solid deck and utterly surprised by the puncturing thrust of her dirk into his windpipe, gurgled as helplessly as a hooked tuna. It took but a quick shove and gravity did its work, making him disappear through the rear wash. The japing birds covered the splash with their noise as if God had made them for this very purpose.

Surely, Benne would smile at her ingenuity even as he recognized the depth of her daring. His lust would be roused, and on that lust, she would sail to the Port of Mobile—his wife be damned—far enough away to sever the apron strings of her mother and the bastard she carried, regardless of who fathered it.

Swiftly, she crossed the deck to deposit Benne's inlaid dirk in the copper slipper. Randall's blood slid as easily off her hand and into the tepid water as his body rolled off the *Mantis*. She ran back, taking care to avoid the slippery oysters of bird shit, and leaned over the rail to smile on her work. Randall was in his final throes, mouth agape, blood floating in an arc around his head as he flailed—unable to call out, unable to breathe, crimson competing with saline blue to contest which would drown the man first.

She counted her quick thinking as a mercy. Without the lightning stab of Benne's knife, Randall would thrash about for minutes fighting the inevitable. There might even be an attempted rescue. Her action was definitely a blessing to him, and the whole business was over in a matter of seconds, a simple execution.

That poor cat probably swam panicked aside the *Mantis*, scrabbling desperately for a toehold before exhausting itself and being swallowed by the sea. Yes, she did Randall a service: payment in kind for his role in their escape. He should have cleaved to the bargain and parted ways at the isles rather than cleaving to her mother, and by proxy entrapping her.

A wave, or perhaps the wake of the *Mantis*, turned Randall, facedown and still, about, and Renny saw the silken strings cording his shoulders through his soaked shirt. Her mother's purse! He wore her mother's purse, damn her for a fool! She hurled her parasol at the sinking target. Renny's screams of frustration, sounding for all the world like screams of terror, silenced the birds and brought the sailors running. She fell into a timely swoon.

***

Ephraim lifted Renny's head into his lap, bringing her round. She spoke in rapid, disjointed snippets as a small gathering of sailors rushed to her side.

"My parasol… slipped… overboard… blood… gone!" she managed between tears and childish gulps for air.

"Get the captain," the purser ordered the very young man who failed to clear the deck of hazards despite his frenzied swabbing. Making a quick sign of the cross, the sailor set off apace. Others hung on the rail, searching the blue expanse for a bobbing head to no avail. Renny allowed the tears to pour, for her

140

grief in losing the purse was genuine. The lack of wealth would certainly frustrate her efforts and make her dependence on Benne more reality than artifice. Her God-ordained opportunity soured almost as rapidly as it presented itself, and she regretted her oversight in the haste to press her advantage. 'Twas a misstep she would not repeat.

Captain Bonneval arrived and regarded her with the cool demeanor befitting his position, especially in moments of emergency. He must not allow his passion to rule even with the young lady, fascinating harlot as she was, clearly in distress. He and Ephraim helped her to her feet.

"Where is your father, child?" he asked with an almost imperceptible pause before the word father.

"In the sea, gone," she choked and began sobbing uncontrollably, shoulders hunching up and down, leaning into him. The captain held her at arm's length, steadying her rather awkwardly. He exchanged a glance with his purser. Ephraim's chin lifted slightly in recognition before peering into the empty sea a moment and making his way forward to find her mother.

"You shall be quite all right," he spoke as he scanned for any sign of the fallen man. Poor bastard, to drown within sight of the destination was a cruel fate to suffer no matter from what the man ran.

"My parasol," she cried as the gulls overhead resumed their noisy onslaught on the rigging and the deck below, the startling event already forgotten. The girl's grief was hardly more convincing than the unfortunate Clemence's vocation as a blacksmith. Whether by luck or worse, the demise of Randall Clemence played to Renny's advantage, a fact that was transparent in her eyes despite the tears spilling in torrents from them.

"I'll get you another parasol, Mouse," he mumbled quietly as he watched Ephraim escorting her mother to the stern. Markedly pale, Cecille Clemence approached her daughter and the captain with the pall of death draining her face of color. She

141

rushed the final steps as her eyes searched frantically for the man who simply disappeared into the void.

"Madame Clemence," he began for there was no gentle way to deliver this news, "Monsieur Clemence is lost."

"It's all lost, Maman," Renny spat with enough venom that Cecille's hand flew to her mouth, stricken. An unearthly sound, the wail of crushing loss and manifest pain, emitted from Cecille's throat before she collapsed to the deck.

***

The young sailor made quick work with his swab as he pushed the puddle of blood found beneath the grieving wife off a wash and moved to the copper slipper to dip enough water to thoroughly rinse away the remnants. He shook his head and crossed himself again to ward off further misfortune. She lost her husband and her baby in the same day. That was a heavy cross to bear. At least she had the pretty young daughter to lean upon and was not as utterly alone as he.

A glittering caught his eye. The sailor reached into the copper slipper and fished out an attractive, inlaid dirk. Normally, he would have pocketed the treasure, but the events of the day and the infernal shitting of those damned shorebirds put him in mind of the labors of Purgatory, and he was in need of absolution. He finished his work and sought out the purser.

The birds absconded immediately after *The Praying Mantis* docked, making their way to refuge in the cashews as swiftly as the passengers crossed the gangplank. Captain Bonneval, ostensibly caring for the grieving family below, did not make an appearance to bid them farewell.

He re-buttoned his breeches as he gave instructions to Renny, who fairly jumped on him in her desperation once her mother fell into the deep sleep induced by a dram of laudanum.

"You shall escort your mother to the sanitarium here on the island. I have already made the arrangements. Take care, my

142

mouse, for it is a leprous place, but she will be treated well. Three days hence, the *Mantis* sails for America. Join me if thou wilt."

"As your wife?" she asked, attempting to pull him back to her.

"You know I am twice married, but, nevertheless…"

"Nevertheless, you shall be thrice married," she stated confidently.

A subtle knock on Benne's door brought their conversation to an end.

"Captain," stated the purser, "the litter has arrived. I have a couple of men waiting to carry Madame Clemence out."

"Well done, Ephraim."

He shooed Renny up the ladder and back to her proper berth. Silently, the purser handed Bonneval the dirk. The seams of the inlay were a telltale brown. The captain nodded, then made ready to greet his island wife.

26

Cecille

She awoke to the strokes of a cool compress tracing the line of her cheekbone and dipping to run her jawline before making the circuit up and across her forehead. An astringent odor, similar to juniper, triggered long-ago memories of an apothecary's chamber. Eyes closed, she explored, opening drawers and fingering herbs with her child's hands as she searched, determination swiftly turning to frantic destruction in her wake. The memory pressed on, despite the dread creeping into her dreamlike consciousness. The woman, long silvered hair flung haphazardly across her stricken face, slumped across a table littered with bottles and parchment, staring sightlessly.

"Non, Maman," murmured Cecille as she shook the memory loose and opened her eyes.

"*Allongez-vous, s'il vous plait.* It is necessary to lie still, Madame," said the mollifying voice attached to the junipered hand. The woman, coifed as a nun, but with skin the rich color of melted chocolate, held compassion in her tone and gentle touch. Cecille's hands moved instinctually toward her womb, which ached deep within despite the medicines she had been given. "Non, Madame, the babe is no more. *Je suis desole.*"

The dark woman continued to trace gentle circles on Cecille's face as she wiped away the tears. "You are compelled to remain here, Madame, until God sees fit to cleanse you of your sins. Absolution may come if you pray consistently. I have seen it on occasion. Until then, you shall have a cell for sleeping and the grounds for your contemplation. You, of course, shall earn your keep after the lying-in." The words stung as the reality of her situation came slowly into focus. Cecille struggled to clear the fog in her mind.

"I am to be imprisoned?" Cecille bristled as she tried to sit up. The firm hand, uncommon in its strength, guided her back in place. "On what charge?"

"Tis no charge but the judgment of the Lord. You are cursed with the *lepre*. The burning of your loins shall serve as a constant testament to your transgressions. Perhaps the lesions shall heal; *peut-etre pas*. I encourage you to pray forgiveness, and I shall pray for your deliverance as I do for all our penitents."

The dark woman's tone matched the gentleness of her sure strokes, but her eyes betrayed a compassion of duty rather than nature.

"Now, Madame, I have some *confort* for you. All is not lost; your daughter is well and here to see you." The dark woman disappeared, and when Cecille opened her eyes again Renny was before her.

"I have come, Maman, to bid you farewell," the girl said evenly, a slight smile tickling the edges of her mouth as she stood over her mother.

"What do you mean?"

"I shall continue onward with the *Mantis*. Life at sea suits me well, I should think."

"Under whose patronage?" Cecille asked, incredulous. "We are penniless. I am ill. We have nothing. Randall is drowned. It is over."

"Yes, Maman, it was rather stupid of you to allow Randall possession of your purse. I saw it just as the sea took him. It prompted me to call out for help."

"What are you saying, daughter?"

"I am informing you, mother, as if you do not already surmise, that 'tis you who is penniless. 'Tis you who is ill. I suspect with a parting vengeance from the man you killed rather than the leper's curse, but no matter. 'Tis you who has nothing!"

145

Cecille's eyes narrowed. "Do not forget, you drove the point that drained that bastard's life. I regret it not, but you bear the burden of the sin along with me."

"I was but a child acting under her mother's tutelage," Renny retorted. "Your instruction did not go unheard, however. Randall, addle-minded as he was, knew the point just as the bastard my father. Do you not think a watery grave is more merciful than a conflagration, Maman?" Renny was smiling, enjoying the precision with which she unraveled the cords of her mother's ambition.

"You killed him!" hissed Cecille, almost apoplectic in her shock. She rose to her elbows, mustering what little strength she had.

"I risked everything to give you a name, a place you were denied. You scoffed at my efforts and threw away my... our... last opportunity for some semblance of peace, of freedom. And for what? We crossed an entire ocean to escape his cruelty, only to find the selfsame bloodlust coursing through your veins."

"Rail on, Maman," Renny responded. "You have done your worst, but it is I who shall persist. You should have made it known he was my father before engaging me in your grisly vengeance. I could have warmed him to me, certainly. I knew him only as a cruel whoremaster, and for that, I shall never forgive you."

"Fool! Yes, I was his whore despite all my efforts. He would have used you just as he used me. He knew you were his blood, and he cared not. I protected you, delivered you from that prison, and now you lock me in another cage?"

"You should be accustomed to it, Maman." Renny's disquieting calm contrasted sharply to Cecille's desperation, a rift as wide as the ocean, parting mother and daughter forever. Cecille turned her back to Renny and spoke to the wall.

"I will never look on you again. Had I the strength to drain his vile blood from your body, I would do so. I know of your harlotry with the captain, you *poubelle*. Depart from me with this as your legacy: you shall never be anything but a whore. I curse you and the daughters you bear. May all your sons bring despair to your icy heart."

"Actually, Maman, I shall be married within days. I shall achieve all that you hoped for whilst you wallow here, alone, with nothing to keep you company save for your empty curse. Goodbye, Maman." Renny rose.

"Why?" whispered Cecille, perhaps to Renny, perhaps to God Himself.

"Oh, Maman," Renny paused for effect, "Whyever not?" She closed the door with a finality befitting the permanence of their parting.

***

Renny made her way toward the quay with a spring in her step and a smile on her lips. She nodded to the dark children tripping barefoot along the cobbles and twirled her new parasol in the sparkling sunlight. A smart sea breeze kept the heat from being oppressive and blew the astringent stench hanging over the sanitarium like a pall away from her. It was quite sporting to move people out of her way. Her mother's abject misery was a balm; she should not miss her at all as she ventured forth.

Renny reached into the pocket of her dress to finger the toy sailing ship that now symbolized yet another facet of the journey to shape her future. She was so pleased with herself that she arrived at the quay quite before she realized. *The Praying Mantis*, sails unfurled, was just crossing the breakers beyond the mouth of the bay.

Part Three

Daughter

North Alabama, 198-

27

Caro

She was already exhausted, both physically and mentally, before this journey truly began. Her mother, the last remaining link to the past, was tucked neatly into the corner of the renovated garage, the hospital bed in stark contrast to the Wild West bar Isom installed last year. Her daughter, the last remaining link to the future, was hollow-eyed and skinny but none the worse for the wear. She would perk up as children always do. Deborah should be thankful she has the luxury of the final days of summer with its heat and humidity that are enough to make eggs sweat even at July Mountain's elevation. School would begin soon enough; but in the meantime, Deborah could soothe herself in air-conditioned comfort with a stack of books.

Caro was glad now she had the foresight to join the mail-order book club in Deborah's name. It only cost a penny and a box of hand-selected novels appeared in the farmhouse mailbox out front. Small as it was, receiving occasional mail would be a pleasure for the girl, some little piece of hope. That mailbox was the only "country" touch Isom approved of without making disparaging remarks about Caro's redneck roots showing. He approved it because it was oversized and Isom liked anything whose size broadcast his importance. Anyone who drove past their extra-large mailbox, gawking at their chocolate-colored house surrounded by its oversized sundeck, would know that here lives a man who expects big things.

The book club sent eight novels, plus two bonus stories, in exchange for Isom's credit card number and an agreement to buy one additional book per month at the already low regular price, automatically charged for the reader's convenience. Caro opened the first package weeks ago, carefully arranging the volumes on a bookshelf she found at an antique store and painted a smart red. It was her coming-home gift—maybe even a peace offering of sorts—for Deborah.

She swallowed the grief that came with Brent's death, choking it down, tamping into her soul so that it became a part of her. A child's death is not something to be gotten over, no matter how many times Isom threatened to send her to the Bryce crazy-house down in Tuscaloosa or to have her hooked up to one of those electro-shock therapy machines if she didn't snap out of it.

He accused her of erasing Brent from their lives like the ancient Egyptians effacing the statues of shamed leaders. He did not want her to grieve openly because people would talk; he did not want her to keep a shrine in Brent's memory or clear his things away, for what would people say? The only thing she was sure of in Isom's labyrinth of "living with a son who's dead" was his blanket disapproval.

He buried Brent in his work, covering him in a shroud of cash washed down in cheap beer. He built a swimming pool, for God's sake, with part of the insurance policy. He used the other part to invest in the stock market, some sort of computer processor that would likely never get off the ground. He told her Brent's money was man's business, and had she been home where she belonged instead of working at that goddamn hospital at a job she didn't even need, Brent would still be here.

She could not live frozen in time any longer. She couldn't sleep, though Isom said she slept too much and was lazy. She couldn't eat, though Isom was quick to note that she gained weight and was piggish. She couldn't persist in this loveless marriage, though Isom said he'd kill her before he granted a divorce. She believed him and swallowed her inadequacies down on top of her grief.

152

She swallowed Darvon, too, pilfered from the locked cabinet at the nurses' station. The thievery offered little comfort and added to her guilt, not so much because stealing is a sin, but because she knowingly and willingly denied an unsuspecting patient part of her prescription. The payoff wasn't worth the risk, not really… three, maybe four hours of dreamless sleep followed by a raging headache…. She told herself she wouldn't do it again, but found herself pocketing a pill when the opportunity presented itself. In her position as the charge nurse, it was almost too easy.

Now as her straight-laced, Bible thumping mother lay ironically in their whiskey-soaked bar recovering from a stroke, Caro found it unnecessary to raid the dosages of hospital patients when she had a supply of narcotics as easy to access as the neatly arranged liquors on the mirrored shelf. Every detail of the bar smacked of authenticity, from the red leather swivel stools to the sanded plank bartop. Isom was nothing if not a details man. The bar itself had seating for ten and was naturally a fully-appointed wet bar. A commercial billiard table complete with an impressively noisy automatic ball return filled the other side of the old garage. The wall was lined with numbered oak chairs Isom had recovered from an old movie theatre or ballpark, she couldn't remember which.

A load bearing pole in the middle of the room was encased top to bottom in a polished oak contraption—part wine rack, part trophy case, part cue stick caddy. On its fourth side, which was solid, Isom hung a whimsical barroom sign reading, "Billiard players, check your balls before entering." The front corner of the room, which was now Nonny's sickroom, featured a loveseat in a smart brown plaid, an oaken console stereo with turntable, 8-track deck, and a cassette player that Isom didn't allow her to touch because electronics are too complicated for women. Never mind that she operates components whose readings spell life or death for patients in the intensive care unit; surely, she can't possibly work out the difference between play and pause.

153

These items were shoved in behind the far side of the bar to make room for the hospital bed and equipment that could easily roll in through the sliding glass door. Caro suspected Isom gave up a little piece of his beloved party room for two reasons: one, he was too damn lazy to haul the hospital bed upstairs to Brent's old room, and two, he knew Nonny would hate everything about the barroom, and this would be a way for him to get back at her for putting them through the inconvenience of her survival.

28

Deborah

Everything changed, yet nothing changed. How could that be? Deborah sat on the cushioned sill of her bay window, cheek pressed to the cool glass and looking out through the pine trees speckling the yard. A copy of *Rebecca* by Daphne Du Maurier rested in her lap, largely unread. She couldn't get past the first sentence.

"Last night I dreamt I went to Manderley again."

The words were powerful. The words were haunting. The words spoke volumes to her in a single statement because they were true. Her dreams, which had returned in the nights leading up to Nonny's fire, followed her to July Mountain. They would be with her always, she realized, because they were a part of her. The dreams were more than imagination. They were memories, played out through eyes that both were and were not hers. The memories did not belong to her, yet their poignancy was bone-deep, maybe even soul-deep.

She opened the book again and tried the line aloud.

"'Last night I dreamt I went to Manderley again'. Last night I dreamt of *Bonny Mantis* again." The new words came from the depths of consciousness accompanied by a sensation of salt air. Deborah remembered a lesson, a wonderful terrible writing lesson, where the teacher had the students sniff the contents of a number of jars.

Miss Kinsee explained that smells were attached to memories and people could make good stories from good smells. She painted the jars black, so the students couldn't guess the contents as they approached and spoil the surprise. The children took turns, sniffing eagerly while obediently closing their real eyes so that the little memory stories could play in their mind's eye. The trick, Miss Kinsee instructed, was to rush back to their seats and write the memory down while the scent was still fresh in their noses. This was one way famous authors found their ideas for stories.

Deborah was in the second wave of students to approach the mysterious jars. The kid in front of her rushed back to his desk grinning, so she expected a pleasant smell. In fact, all the children were having fun, so Miss Kinsee must have picked good-smelling items for happy little memoirs. Deborah closed her eyes and took a hefty whiff of chocolate. Instantly, she gagged on loamy soil and fear. The rush of angry wind filled her ears. The next thing she knew, Miss Kinsee was lifting her to her feet and sending her to the water fountain.

"You must have smelled too hard, Deborah!" Miss Kinsee chastised. She allowed Deborah to put her head down on the desk instead of writing a memoir. Deborah kept her head down as she listened to her classmates read their paragraphs describing fun times at the county fair, holidays, and sweet treats they enjoyed. They weren't even stories, really, but Miss Kinsee carried on like the kids were Newberry Award winners.

It was the first time Deborah felt keenly different from other children, not just smarter but a weirdo as well. She felt different from her teacher, too. Miss Kinsee was wrong. Good stories didn't come from good smells; those were just memories. Her lesson was babyish, if you could see past the novelty of getting to smell a mysterious odor that even a toddler would recognize. The good stories come from the bad memories, the ones you can't share at school.

156

Deborah shook herself from her reverie and thought about the words she just transposed from du Maurier, seeping up from her mind like those bubbles at the tar pits in California. Maybe one day she could see those pits for herself, but for now it was enough to watch the breeze blowing through the pines. From her cool perch, the outdoors looked inviting, but it was a false impression. The wind through the pines blew hot, and upon close inspection, the trunks bled sap as they sweated in the sun. "Last night I dreamt of *Bonny Mantis* again," Deborah whispered. Was *Bonny Mantis* the name of a ship? *Her* ship?

"Deborah! Deb!" her mother called from downstairs. "Put down your book and come get some lunch. I need you to help feed Nonny." Deborah read the opening line one more time. If the fictional Rebecca was haunted by dreams, maybe the real-life Deborah wasn't alone. What if Rebecca was crazy, though, and the dreams meaningless? There was no blurb on the back of the book to guide her, only praise from important newspapers and such. It agitated her when nothing on the back cover of a book talked about the story inside. Deborah made the decision not to read the book, at least, not yet. She buried it between *The Adventures of Huckleberry Finn* and *The Heart Is a Lonely Hunter* on her new red bookcase, but that opening line lay embossed on her mind, an entire novel… no, an entire memoir in a single sentence.

***

The quiet of home grated on Deborah and she longed for the noisiness that comes with junior high school. She counted down the days until seventh grade began, not because she was looking forward to seeing friends—she had none—but because it would offer respite from the deafening quiet on July Mountain. Ambient sound, of course, was all around: squirrels chirping outside, Nonny's equipment whirring in rhythm to her raspy breath, pine needles sweeping against one another in the breeze.

157

Mom worried that Nonny might be developing pneumonia and was sneaking snorts of whiskey into Nonny's medicine, knowing Nonny would never willingly drink. She took a snort for every one she administered to Nonny, so she must have been worried about the pneumonia catching. Mom wasn't so worried that she treated Deborah, though. More likely, Mom was just getting snookered. Her daddy, after all, was an alcoholic according to Nonny. In health class she learned that alcoholism passes down from parent to child. Maybe that meant she would be an alcoholic when she grew up. There were worse things she could do.

Deborah found herself thinking about those worse things a lot in the loneliness of the mountain house. Daddy didn't talk much to Mom; Mom didn't talk much to Nonny; Nonny didn't talk much to Deborah. Absolutely no one uttered the name Brent. It was like he never ran shrieking down the hall, tackling her, shoving her face into the pile carpet while he positioned himself to fart on her head.

Part of the ambient sound surrounding her was the constant chatter of TVs. Daddy decided they needed a TV in most every room of the house. She wouldn't be surprised to find a screen mounted in the bathroom if he kept up his pace. She was surrounded by noise, but living in the silence of loneliness. Talking was a constant, but she had no one to talk to, except of course in the dreams, and even they weren't exactly her own.

Deborah spooned mashed pork and beans mixed up with mayonnaise into Nonny's mouth. The juice from the pork and beans, which Mom poured right out of the can and into a bowl, caused the mayonnaise to separate nauseatingly as it was stirred. Deborah kept wiping the slack side of Nonny's mouth to keep from having to look at the dribble threatening to run down her chin and into the creases of her neck. Mom said taking care of Nonny was like taking care of an oversized baby. She would have to relearn how to do practically everything, and in the meantime, it was up to her and Deborah to do for Nonny.

"A lot of water's run under the bridge, Deborah," explained Mom. "Sometimes that water runs clear and refreshing, other times it is deep and murky. Sometimes it stagnates so that you don't think you can drink it, you know, take another sip of what's being offered to you. Other times, you'd just about rather thirst to death than go back to it. Maybe it's pride. Maybe it's just plain being tired. Maybe it's meanness. Do you see what I'm saying?"

"I'm not sure, Mom."

"Well, let me try it another way. Nonny had you read the Good Book while you were staying with her, didn't she?"

"Yes. It was all she would let me read."

"I figured. That's why I had a whole collection a-waiting on you when you got back home. Do you remember that part about Jesus carrying his cross through the streets of Jerusalem?"

Deborah nodded. "Well, you're old enough to know now that life is a lot like that." Mom lifted her chin toward Nonny, already farting beans while napping through her oxygen treatment.

"There were times when I hated Nonny. There will be times when you hate me. But she's my mother, and I'm yours, for better or worse. We are each other's cross to bear. That's what keeps us sane and what drives us crazy—the weight of it all, all the shit we have to put up with. Running away don't help. Drinking don't help. Pills don't help." Mom was talking more to herself than to Deborah now, but Deborah drank it all in nonetheless. She was so thirsty for conversation.

"You can't escape the cross. Some days it's an easy yoke and others you think it's going to crush you, but it's with you always. You may think you'd be better off dead, or that Nonny would be better off dead, suffering as she is right now. But she's a tough old bird, and she's raised us both to be strong enough to bear that damned cross, especially if we carry it together. Will you do that, Deborah? Will you help me tote our cross?"

159

Deborah couldn't quite grasp what Mom was getting at. "What about Daddy? Isn't he strong enough? He could help us until Nonny gets better."

"I don't mean literally, Little Debbie. Haven't you listened to a word I've said?" Mom only resorted to the childish nickname when condescending. "I swear, sometimes it's like talking to a fence post. You're supposed to be smart, girl. The school says you're gifted." She laughed off the insult. "They don't know the half of it, do they?"

Mom sat down on the hospital bed and started massaging Nonny's legs to keep the circulation going so she wouldn't get bedsores. She didn't even grimace at the stench released when she pulled up the covers. If Nonny's guts were working fine, Caro would have her up and functioning again before much longer.

"Let me spell it out for you so that maybe you can be spared some heartache later on down the line. That's what I want for you, you know. I want you to be spared, but I know better. We all got a cross to bear: Nonny, our mothers before her, me, and you. We're all tied together by blood and history, mother to daughter on and on. So, no matter what's happened in the past, when it comes down to it, we do for each other. That's what family means. We women carry the cross."

"But, Mom, the cross killed even Jesus," Deborah said.

"Just the man-part, Deborah. Nobody, not even Jesus, promised life would be easy. We gotta put one foot in front of the other and carry that cross onward. Right now, that cross is weighted down with Nonny's stroke, the fire, and all that's happened." She couldn't give voice to Brent's name; she swore to herself she'd never speak it again. It was too much.

"The trick to life, Deborah, is to not add weight to your cross if you can help it. Don't go chasing ghosts, dear."

Mom tucked Nonny's veiny legs back under the covers, rose, and kissed Deborah on top of the head. Nonny reached out with her working hand to grasp her daughter's arm. For just a moment, daughter, mother, and grandmother were connected, rooted and unified in unspoken agreement. It was a rare and intimate gesture.

29

Isom

Things were better with Little Debbie back on the mountain. Routines made sense again. He could lean into expectations... of supper, of her ready smile and hug when he got home from the store, of her beautiful face bent close to the pages of a book. She probably needed glasses, but he hoped she could get along without them.

All a girl needed as she entered junior high school was a pair of glasses to ruin her social life before she even had a chance to get it started. Just like no boy in his right mind would look twice at a scraggly-headed girl, one certainly wouldn't look at a four-eyed girl, even if her eyes were the most arresting he'd ever seen. Debbie's hair would grow back nice. She would be a looker by high school. If it came to it, he would pay for expensive contacts for her. He couldn't bear to have an ugly daughter.

He was embarrassed enough by Caro, who was putting on weight. He tried to talk some sense into her, but she was hell-bent on eating her way through her grief. He even cleared the cabinets of cookies and chips, making a show of just how many calories were in a serving. She just sat and took his rant, eyes dull and focused elsewhere.

He got so mad a chip bag exploded in his hands, sending barbeque chips all over the carpeted kitchen floor. Almost before he realized what he was doing, he found himself manhandling her to the floor, forcing chips into her mouth.

"If you're going to eat everything in sight, you can be a goddamned vacuum and clean this shit up!" he yelled in her ear.

He had her by the scruff of the neck, pushing her face into the carpet of crushed chips.

When at last he released her, she sat back on her haunches, looked him dead in the eye and said, "Mmm. That was good."

That was the first time he backhanded her.

***

He still wasn't sleeping, and the beer seemed to rile him up instead of lull him like it used to. He roamed the house at night, his wanderings masked by the TVs which stayed on long after the national anthem played and they went to white noise. He kept them on especially in the dead of night because he couldn't stand the silence. It made him think of how quiet it must be inside Brent's grave, how dark.

He just signed on a new tenant at the strip mall; one of those new satellite dishes would allow him to get programs at all hours. It was crazy to sit and watch snowstorms or those humming rainbow stripes on the screen. Besides, the damn dog, Samson, hadn't shut up at night in weeks. He was running something in the woods damn near every night. He was far enough off not to be loud, but the incessant barking was still annoying as hell.

Isom hadn't handled his pistol since fetching Little Debbie from Nonny's house. Served the old bitch right her house burned to the ground after all she'd put Caro through in the past. No wonder his wife was messed up. Of course, the joke was really on him because now the old bag was holed up in his Wild West bar until God knows when. Hopefully, she'll either die or get better soon. He could move her to Debbie's old bedroom, so pink it's like the inside of a bottle of bismuth. Hell would freeze over before he put her in Brent's room. No one would sleep in that room again if he had anything to say about it.

He walked silently on bare feet into the new wing of the house where Little Debbie slept in her tower at the top of the stairs just like a fairytale princess. He crawled up the stairs on all fours, making sure not to put his weight on the fourth step which creaked even though he had the contractor out to repair it twice and threatened a breach of contract suit when the son of a bitch refused to return a third time. He paid good money for this addition, top dollar in fact. He should expect perfection... *house settling, my ass*. He stared down the offensive step as he avoided it and silently cussed the contractor.

The door at the top of the stairs was only partially closed. Isom slowly opened it enough so that he could look in on her slumber. The moon cast a steady beam through the skylight, bisecting her bed like a coverlet from the sky. Her face relaxed in darkness, but her torso was illuminated by the soft light, naked alabaster perfection.

She must have gotten too warm as she slept, tossing her T-shirt carelessly to the floor. He found himself blushing, but he could not look away for several minutes. Finally, some shift in the clouds hid the moon's light and broke the spell. Isom crept silently back down the stairs and into the sunroom. Samson stood guard just outside the window, eyeing him and growling low. That dog needed a lesson. He needed another beer.

30

Nonny

She just knew Isom set her up in the bar out of pure tee spite. Braining himself on that step may have killed Levin when he had no business being at that little shithole of a house Caro married into to start with, but that was just because the fall beat the alcohol to him. He was already well on his way to drinking himself into the grave. The alcohol would get Isom, too, in the end. Judging by the rows and rows of booze she had to look at every time the fog of medication lifted, he would be lucky to see sixty. Isom was high-strung as a banty rooster, dead set on fluffing out his feathers and crowing to all who would hear what a big man he was. Nonny didn't know what Caro saw in the sawed-off son of a bitch and she let her know about it, too. That's why Caro cut her off those years.

She made the effort to make it up to her, though, because that was the Christian thing to do. It looked bad at Social Circle not to be able to chime in with the latest news of children and grandchildren, so she decided she needed to put up with Isom. Caro hoed her row, and now she was reaping what she sowed.

The central air conditioning in the fancy house Isom built was the perfect conduit between the master bedroom and her sickroom below. Nonny heard plenty of hard words raining down over her head deep in the nights since her stroke. Isom hadn't struck Caro, as far as she knew, but he was a mean drunk just like Levin and her daddy before him. It was just a matter of time.

Folks are willing to put up with an awful lot when that's all they know; she was just as guilty as her own mother, her daughter, and likely her granddaughter once she decided to marry. The women in the family could line up a room full of men and head straight for the biggest assholes of the lot. Hell, they could probably pick them out blindfolded without even asking them to bend over.

Her grandson's death made Isom meaner. He wanted to put her away in a nursing home—said everybody would be better off—but Caro was holding her ground and caring for her with a gentleness neither expected nor deserved. The stroke near about killed her. The Lord may have cracked open the Pearly Gates, but she wasn't stepping inside, not yet. Her home was burnt to the ground, but that didn't make her pay much nevermind; it was a cold house full of bitter memories, and she was frankly glad to be shed of it.

As long as she could keep the insurance money out of Isom's pocket, she might be able to make a fresh start once she got well. As long as she could keep that damned ghost off of her granddaughter, the girl might have a shot at finding some happiness. She might as well be blowing dandelions in the wind, but fighting looked a hell of a lot better than growing bedsores and waiting to die.

***

Slowly, as Nonny regained control over her obstinate limbs and she changed her make-up to camouflage the droop of her eyelid, which she suspected may be a permanent souvenir from her stroke, the light returned to Deborah's eyes. School turned the girl's attention outside of herself. She seemed to have shot up in the last month, perky breasts appearing almost overnight.

Isom took her to get a "grown-up" haircut, and her hair was frozen in spray-finished feathered wings that met at the back of her head. Caro had a screaming fit at that, saying he'd turned her into the tart of the seventh grade, but Nonny thought it was a darling haircut. So darling, in fact, that she almost forgot how much she disliked Isom and caught herself smiling in approval.

Her own hair was frightening enough to raise the dead and there wasn't a damn thing she could do with it aside from braiding it in pigtails like some sort of pruned-up Indian school girl. She still couldn't hold up her slack arm for long enough to be worth anything. She even thought about calling Mrs. Garlan and offering her ten dollars extra if she'd drive to July Mountain to come set her hair.

"Fool, old woman!" Nonny said to her reflection in the bathroom mirror, "How the hell are you gonna climb them stairs to the phone? And just how do you intend to call your hairdresser who burnt up a-snooping around your house? Thy, Lord!"

Nonny laughed at herself while she made her way from the tiny bathroom back toward her bed. The short hallway was narrow enough to catch her and keep her from falling if she toddled on her cane. Navigating the stairs was an impossibility. Even crossing the threshold into her quarters was dicey. Her slack foot didn't want to raise high enough for her to keep from dragging her toe. She worried incessantly about falling.

Caro brought her meals, administered her medicine, and kept her in clean nightgowns, but didn't really keep company. She helped her in and out of the tub twice a week with that clinical detachment nurses use on patients, not family. Her daughter had healing in her hands, but it stopped there. She did her duty, and she did it well. If it weren't for her granddaughter breathing life into the house, Nonny might as well be in a nursing home. At least she would have other old folks to talk to and maybe play a few hands of spades.

Living in a makeshift pool hall was surely a temptation put before her by the Lord, or maybe it was a punishment for her failure to bring Deborah to Him despite filling her with His Word. But there was time yet, and Nonny believed for every purpose there is a reason. She was bored and lonely. She missed her talks with Levin out at the cemetery. They had better

167

conversations with six feet of dirt between them than they ever had wrapped up together with nothing but a quilt.

She missed her routines. As the trauma of the stroke abated, she needed normalcy again, not this marking time between meals and dosages. Her mind was mobile, but her limbs restricted. She realized she took her health for granted. That's why God took it from her. She would take it back, fight for it. She wasn't about to let Him end her this way.

Folks ought to have some say in how they want to meet their maker. Otherwise, what was the use in His giving everybody free will? If the Lord wanted a bunch of robots, he would have made a bunch of robots instead of thinking, feeling, fire-pissing folks. She'd been through enough hell in her lifetime to know a thing or two about pissing fire. She may have been dealt a hand with no face cards, but by God, she'd play her damn deuces for all they were worth.

Nonny looked to the laundry basket full of socks Caro left on her bed this morning.

"This will be good practice for you. You want to be able to get along by yourself, don't you? I want you to sort out these socks and ball up the pairs. It's good exercise and will help you get stronger," Caro instructed.

"Now, remember Isom likes the socks to be all-the-way balled up like little grenades. Don't let the toes hang out like you always done back home. That won't do for Isom. He's particular about laundry."

"He's particular about a lot of things," replied Nonny.

Caro ignored the jab.

"I expect these socks to be sorted and rolled when I bring your lunch. It's time you got out of the bed and back into earning your keep."

Caro turned to leave.

"Caroline Clemm?" She watched her daughter's shoulders stiffen. Caro stopped without turning back to face Nonny.

168

"I'm still your mother. I'd like to talk with you."
"Oh, Mother. We ran out of things to say years ago."

31

Deborah

Deborah reported to Nonny each afternoon after she got off the school bus and worked her way past Samson the bulldog. Since she returned home, the dog seemed confused. He growled low and mean, the hairs on his back bristling and his front paws wide in a defensive stance. It was like Samson forgot who she was, or maybe mistook her, until she could coax him into a halting calm with her voice.

She would supervise while Nonny made deliberate laps around the pool table with her cane, another souvenir from her stroke. While Nonny walked, Deborah would read aloud from the Bible, and Nonny would provide color commentary, almost like Howard Cosell on *The Wide World of Sports*. In the Good Book, just like in life, some folks felt the thrill of victory while others suffered the agony of defeat.

Deborah wanted to laugh at Nonny's comments, but she wasn't sure how Nonny would react. Deborah was not allowed to put any personality into her biblical readings whatsoever, speaking in a sleepy monotone befitting the gravity of the words. The time she tried to spice things up a bit, she was met with a long, boring lecture on the dangers of hellfire for defaming the holy unadulterated word of God.

This afternoon was different, however, as Mom gave her some bizarre instructions and a laundry basket full of balled-up socks.

"Deborah, Nonny has to be put to work now that she's improving. I want you to take this basket and dump these socks out all around the floor, just like you're throwing Easter eggs on the ground for a baby to find. Nonny's gotta pick up all them sock balls and put them back in the basket, which I want you to set in the far corner of the room."

"Won't she fall and hurt herself, tripping on socks?"

"Not with you watching over her. The only way to regain the strength in her affected limbs is to work them. She's decided not to die, so that means it's our job to help her get better. She's not going to like it, but all that squatting is good for her."

"I have homework," Deborah protested. The idea of listening to Nonny gripe about picking up socks was too much to bear, especially since she had read ahead in English class. They were plodding through *The Adventures of Tom Sawyer* and her classmates were all a-titter about whether Tom was going to kiss Becky Thatcher in that cave. The boys were still talking about how smart Tom was to sucker all the kids into painting his fence and bragging about how they would have seen right through Tom's scam and whacked him one upside the head maybe even with his own paintbrush. She laughed at the bravado of a bunch of boys who were still sounding out words, but the idiots thought she was laughing in agreement with them. They were sheep, every one.

She wouldn't give two cents for Tom Sawyer, but Huckleberry Finn? Now, he was an interesting character. Mark Twain must have thought along the same lines because he wrote a whole 'nother book about Huck, and she had it right there on her red shelf. Deborah was anxious to get to it, especially since her idiot teacher said it was too advanced for a seventh grader.

"You're right, Missy, and your homework is to do your part right here at home."

Mom handed Deborah the basket and spun her toward the stairs leading to what Deborah secretly called "The Nonny Dungeon." Deborah sighed. Huckleberry Finn would have to take a number. Maybe Nonny would choose a decent Bible story this afternoon. The past couple of afternoons she had to read a long list of stupid, pointless rules that don't even apply to the modern world and another list of begats where Nonny corrected her pronunciation on every other name. It was lame, but so was Nonny. Deborah smiled at her clever pun.

If she could speed up Nonny's healing, she would have more free time to read, and maybe they could move Nonny out of her trollish lair in Daddy's saloon. Daddy would like that. She overheard him mutter something about his barroom smelling like old lady powder farts. Her mood was already lightened before she stepped in to engage her grandmother in an extended game of fetch.

Nonny said, "If I have to pick up all these durn socks, I want to hear a fitting story. Open up the King James to Second Corinthians, I believe near about Chapter 12."

Deborah couldn't recall any story from the Bible that had to do with gathering up socks, but she rushed to find the correct spot in the Good Book. Nonny berated her if she couldn't find random chapters on command, telling her that if she had Jesus in her heart she'd know His word well enough to find it when it was requested of her. Deborah became adept at flipping quickly to whatever book Nonny barked out.

Nonny knew the Bible backwards and forwards and could quote chapter and verse so accurately that Deborah wondered why she even wanted her to read aloud. She could probably recite it cover to cover. Nonny certainly was quick to correct Deborah if she misspoke at all, and even when she was bored stiff with reading and Nonny appeared to nod off, her grandmother would snap to attention if she skipped even a phrase.

"Alright, gal, you get to reading, and I'll get to grabbing," Nonny directed.

Deborah sat up on the pool table, taking extra care not to scratch the green carpet with the rivets on the back pockets of her jeans. Daddy took so much pride in the quality of his pool table he threatened to whip Brent's ass if he scratched it up. She was always extra careful around it. Nonny hiked up her housedress, knotting it up above her knees and pushed the sleeves up above her elbows. Using her cane, she launched a sock ball toward the basket waiting in the corner.

"Two points!" she laughed.

"Nonny, that's not what Mom said you're supposed to do," Deborah grinned.

"Your mom says a lot of things at me, but rarely to me, so I'll exercise the way I damn well please." This time the sock ball went wide right.

"You won't get better unless you squat. Don't you want to get out of here?"

"And go where? You done burnt my house down." Nonny said this with a twinkle in her eye so that it was more like a fact than an accusation. She launched a sock just past Deborah's head.

"Now, read me some scripture, gal, and I'll squat like a chicken dropping eggs."

"Yes, ma'am, but you can't throw 'em at the basket; you've got to walk them over to it, one at a time," Deborah was actually having fun. Seeing Nonny in a playful mood, conspiring with her about her mama, and smiling instead of scowling was a welcome surprise.

Deborah assumed her Bible-reading voice, keeping close tabs on Nonny out of the corner of her eye.

"For though I would desire to glory, I shall not be a fool; for I will say the truth: but now I forbear, lest any man should think of me above that which he seeth me to be, or that he heareth of me."

"Peter, Paul, and Mary!" exclaimed Nonny. "That man is talking in circles already. He wants glory; well, don't we all? But he don't want folks giving him credit for glory. He wants to tell the truth, but he's scared the truth will make folks think too much of him. That's one prideful humble man right there, what with

173

him being a doctor and all, it's no wonder he had the devil of putting on airs. He was a smart man, maybe too smart for his own good, like a certain seventh grader I know."

Nonny's commentary, funny as it could be, always pointed back at Deborah, her parents, or "those Pharisees and Sadducees up in Washington, D.C." For Nonny, the Bible was as real as Sunday Meeting and applied directly to everyone else's lives like either a salve or a stinging antiseptic, according to Nonny's mood and interpretation of the Word. She was getting worked up today as she bent to pick up those sock balls and dutifully hobbled them over to the basket. Deborah wasn't sure she would get too many verses in edgewise. At least the reading would be short. Nonny would tire herself out at this pace.

> "And lest I should be exalted above measure
> through the abundance of the revelations, there
> was given to me a thorn in the flesh, the
> messenger of Satan to buffet me, lest I should be
> exalted above measure."

"Good Lord-a-Livin', girl! Can't you read? That's buffet, not buf-fay like the Lord has set a table before his enemies piled up with barbeque, tater salad, slaw, and all the fixin's! You're supposed to be smart. Now read it again right. Buf-fay. What in the world are they teachin' down at that school? Shore ain't readin' skills. Set to, Deborah."

Deborah read the verse again, being sure to pronounce buffet the way Nonny said. King James was a chore to read, but Nonny wouldn't have any other version. She believed only the King James was the true word of God. Deborah didn't dare comment on Jesus speaking the King's English back in the Bible days.

> "And lest I should be exalted above measure
> through the abundance of the revelations, there
> was given to me a thorn in the flesh, the

174

messenger of Satan to buffet me, lest I should be exalted above measure."

"Deborah, did you hear the words you just read? Old Doctor Paul gets me worked up about his ego... 'lest I should be exalted,' my foot. That man wants all the exaltation we can throw at him. He's just like one of them high school girls lined up hoping to be crowned Homecoming Queen. 'Oh, I never imagined I would be elected.' Foot! She imagined it alright, right down to waving to her adoring crowd at the parade with that crown a-twinkling on her pretty head."

"Nonny, were you the Homecoming Queen?"

"Nah. You, your mama, and me? We ain't Homecoming Queen ilk. That's what I was getting to. The truth of the Lord's Word is hid up right in between Paul's 'lests,', and it explains a lot about the lot we Clemm women drew in this world."

Deborah rested the Bible on her lap. If she were lucky, she was already done with her reading, because Nonny was about to preach. In fact, she was pretty certain that if Nonny had the good fortune to be made a man instead of a woman, she would have made a preacher. She had all the best preacher qualities: she liked to talk, she could dress a person down with guilt, or judge them silently with condescension. She knew the Bible backwards and forwards but didn't have a clue what it really meant.

Deborah didn't know what all it meant, either, but she figured that was the point. People aren't supposed to know what all it means. How can folks be expected to believe in miracles if they don't have mysteries? She thought briefly of *Huckleberry Finn* waiting for her upstairs. It would be awesome to just float down the Mississippi without worrying about old ladies throwing Bible verses at you like darts or having to struggle with figuring out what God thinks is right. She bet Huck would have it made. Nowadays, they don't let boys run free like that. Girls never have run free, and Deborah reckoned they never will.

A sock ball pegged her right between the eyes.

"Here I am imparting the wisdom of the ages on the undeserving likes of you. The least you can do is pay attention," Nonny scolded. "Now, that thorn in the flesh. You know about that thorn, always digging into your innards for a sticking place. Sometimes she works her way out of your skin, and that's when she smarts the most. But try as you might, you can't tweeze her out. Some part is always left behind, a sore spot down deep where she'll root until she eats her way to the surface again."

"Who are you talking about, Nonny?"

"You know damn well who I'm talking about. It says so right there in the Bible: 'the messenger of Satan.' She's our thorn in the flesh, a part of us put there by God to test our mettle or temper our happiness. I don't know which, and I don't know why and probably won't this side of Heaven. The Lord's got some explaining to do when He's ready for me. She's as much a part of us, our history, as our name, and she's got a mighty strong hold on your soul, girl."

Nonny continued. "She feeds on two things: innocence and contentment. She just gnaws away on the inside biding her time, sometimes for decades, until she strikes with the sudden fury of a snake, like one of them water moccasins that will chase after you out of nothing but evil. She took your brother. She took my son. She takes time and again. She will take you if you let her."

"She came the night of the fire," Deborah whispered.

"Yes, because you opened the door with your meddling."

"I didn't mean to."

"Of course you did. You couldn't stop yourself. And you can't stop her, not forever because she is forever. She's as old as our name."

"Then let's throw it away."

"Now you listen here, Deborah, and you let this burn in real good. Our name is our connection, our link to the past and to the future. Throwing away your name won't work because who you are is in your blood, in mine. There's protection in your name just as there is despair. Don't turn your back on the name, and, for

176

God's sake, don't fail to bestow our name on your daughter when the time comes. It will keep her just like it has kept you."

Nonny's face was flushed and a little spittle perched on her chin as she spoke, threatening to drop on Daddy's pool table. "Now read that next verse. God provides an answer to our problem."

Deborah picked up where she left off. They'd drifted a long way from Paul's letter, but Nonny was about to connect it all together.

> "For this thing I besought the Lord thrice, that
> it might depart from me. And he said unto me, My
> grace is sufficient for thee."

"Do you see? You can ask the Lord again and again to take this affliction away, but you're stuck with it. He isn't going to take her away, because she is a part of who we are, like it or not. She is your thorn in the flesh, and when the Lord demands his pound, it won't be from the chunk she's worming her way through. It will be from the chunk you hold most dear. Do you understand, Little Debbie? You have to just put up with it. You can't throw it away. If you do that, we are all lost."

Little Debbie, God how she hated that stupid name, didn't see at all. Nonny was old, on medication, and all mixed up in her interpretations of the Bible. Her grandmother ageless was a demon set on destroying everything she loved or would love, and Nonny thought this was the will of God? Her mother buried all her feelings with Brent. Her father was an enigma of callousness and warmth. She was haunted by dreams that didn't even belong to her. She'd spent the spring and most of the summer reading nothing but the Bible. If God's big message was to "put up with it," then to hell with Him.

32

Isom

The routine of school, a decent haircut, and a brand new set of titties really brought Little Debbie around. Now, if he could get Caro to agree to some mascara and lip gloss she could cover that spooky look about her. Caro, though, thought seventh grade was too early for makeup and the like. She was wrong.

It wouldn't hurt her to slap on a little herself around the house. She used to look real pretty with that silvered hair flowing down and those bright eyes, but now she looked like a frumpy housewife, ankles thickening by the day and hair yanked back in a goddamned bun. Well, she may have let herself go to hell, but he'd be damned if he'd send his daughter there with her.

He made an appointment at the local makeup shop for Saturday morning so she could get a proper lesson since Caro damn well wasn't going to do her duty as a mother. Damn Nonny didn't miss a day, though. She was laid up in his bar with so much eye makeup on she looked like a washed-up saloon whore. How a mother and daughter could be so different was beyond him. No wonder his girl looked a little flighty when she didn't know anyone was watching.

No, it was up to him to make something of his Little Debbie. She had too many pretty qualities to waste if he could get her out from under those damned female influences. A little makeup should do the trick. He would sign her up for cheerleader tryouts in the spring. She would look gorgeous in one of those short skirts up on top of a pyramid, all those other girls looking up and wishing they were her. He would hire a gym trainer to teach her how to do one of those back handsprings, and she'd be set.

For now, he needed to turn her attention away from all those books. She didn't need to be cooped up in the house reading to Nonny, who was milking her damn stroke for all it was worth, only to closet herself in her room and read some more. Most nights when he checked on her, she had a novel neatly downturned on the pillow beside her head. A good metal detector should get her out and about. Besides, he wanted one for himself as well. They could go on expeditions out around that old site of the burnt down hotel across the ridge or to that cave on the back side of the mountain, just the two of them.

With fall settling in, Isom pulled the cover over his pool to close it until next spring. Caro ought to be over him using the insurance money to put it in and they can host parties when the weather warms back up. Everyone likes a girl with a pool. Little Debbie will invite her cheer squad over and the girls can all take turns modeling their bikinis down the diving board runway. Of course, he will buy her the prettiest swimsuits. Her compact legs will be tanned, and her cleavage will peep just enough out of the triangle top to be kissed by the sun. She will be beautiful, and he will make her so.

It was football season, and finally the weather agreed. In North Alabama, entire towns fill stadiums to watch their boys try to take each other's heads off. Over the course of the season, players and fans witness the weather swing from the threat of heat stroke in the early games to bitterly cold temperatures in the playoffs. It's a tough game that demands both blood and sweat from its players as well as endurance from the fans in the stands. Parades and bragging rights become treasured memories, and a solid hit or a game-saving touchdown can connect a young man with as much opportunity as a college degree. If a boy is good enough to play college ball, he can attain unparalleled status as a demigod in his hometown. Old men sit whittling on the

179

courthouse steps and relive fifty-year-old victories as if they were yesterday.

If anything defines a community, gives it a lasting identity, it's the high school football team. Isom would never be truly accepted in the private clubs and echelons of Scottsboro's elite because he wasn't a Wildcat. Hell, he didn't even play ball in high school, but he kept that under wraps. Brent's athleticism would have opened doors for the both of them. The accident snapped these hopes as abruptly as it snapped Brent's neck. It was all over instantly. Nevertheless, Isom would not miss a game. He would sit and cheer on other men's sons because it was good for business. He would offer the hardest-hitting boy a modest scholarship in Brent' s memory, and in this way, he could carve a piece of the respect in this one-horse town his success couldn't buy.

When that brisk snap of helmets on pads echoed in a crisp staccato on a Friday night, it was also a sure sign the snakes made their way back into holes and rotten tree stumps to lie dormant for the winter. July Mountain had more than its fair share of snakes wriggling around in the leaves. Rattlers and copperheads were the meanest, and Isom didn't allow his kids to roam the woods in the warm weather months without him. He could dispatch them with his pistol.

If wading through snakes weren't enough, the big brown wood spiders hung invisibly at eye level. Nothing was worse than a nasty spider sitting on your face and trying to outrun you to your hairline before you could sweep it off. Damn Brent near about knocked him cold one day when he instinctively swung his baseball bat to ward off a spider. Isom whipped him with his belt. He wished he were still here to scare up more spiders and snakes, clash helmets, and even get more whippings. Isom hated being the father of a dead son.

His daughter, however, was very much alive. With a few changes, she could become his pride and joy. She just needed some air, to get out of the stifling presence of her depressed

180

mother and delusional grandmother. He brought up the idea of a nursing home for Nonny again, knowing full well Caro was dead-set against it. He couldn't understand her. She had trouble breathing the same air as her mother but flat out refused to leave her to anyone else's care.

"Deborah needs to get out more, walk around in the sunshine. You're turning her into a vampire making her babysit your mother," he said.

"I need the break, and Nonny needs the company," Caro responded.

"A break from what? You sure seem to be taking your sweet time getting her up and around. I want her out of my barroom and I want Deborah out of her clutches."

"It's only a few more months, Isom. These things take time. I will move her into the pink bedroom when she can navigate the stairs safely. I'm sure you don't want her falling and breaking a hip. You'd never be rid of her then."

"I could sell her Chrysler. It looks tacky parked in our driveway. We could use the money for a down payment on a nursing home and some diet pills for you," Isom said evenly and turned up a can of beer. He drained it and crushed the can, tossing it on the dresser.

"Don't. It's all she has left; that and the antique lamp pull she hoards like treasure. We owe it to her because she's all the family I have left."

"I don't owe her squat. She never cared a lick for me, and I sure as hell ain't going out of my way to care for her. The nursing home is more for your benefit than it is for hers. You need to get ahold of yourself, Caro. You have to let yourself move on. She's lording over you again, and now she's lording over Deborah. Do you want Deborah to turn out like you? Look at yourself!" He spun his wife to face the dresser, its mirror reflecting her sorrow and a wild look in his eye. She turned to face him, but he forced her head around to confront her reflection.

181

"I said look at yourself. Where's your makeup?" He pinched her cheeks hard so that the color rose. He ripped her hair down so that it fell in a thin sheet past her shoulders. She stood frozen in place, braced for his next move. "You used to be beautiful. Look at yourself. Look at the fat dripping off your arms. I bet I'm the laughing stock of the town. How does any man as successful as I am deserve a wife that looks like this? You turn my stomach. You should be ashamed to be seen."

Caro just took the onslaught, like she just took her mother's disapproval, like she just took whatever abuse he threw her way. It wasn't even satisfying anymore. She was like the damn dog Samson, tail tucked when he had anything to say, a growl of protest low and deep, barely audible.

"I've only gained ten pounds, Isom. I will go on a diet if you'll let me keep my mother these months. It's time for her medicine. I need to go downstairs."

"You'll fix yourself up, and you'll let Deborah fix herself up. Deborah won't be spending her afternoons in a sickroom anymore, either." He spoke to her as she headed out the bedroom door. Isom turned back to the mirror and wiped his face to remove the wild expression. "You're the man. Be the man, Isom," he told his reflection, which looked so much like his father's, and walked to the kitchen to get another cold beer.

182

33

Deborah

It was strange. She no longer spent the afternoons when she got off the bus reading to Nonny, but was given a quick snack and sent outdoors to do as she pleased. She spent the hours between school and supper mostly wandering about, pretending to hunt treasure with that silly metal detector, reading whatever book she had secreted away, and chiefly avoiding Samson. He just plain didn't like her anymore, and she had no idea why. He sniffed and blustered and looked menacingly at her from the corner of his eye. He didn't used to be this way.

Mom kept foisting makeup on her. "Here's some mascara. Be sure you don't glob it up on your lashes. Remember, too much is as tacky as too little," she instructed.

Deborah wasn't much interested in looking like a young lady, but she wasn't much interested in anything but books and learning. Her gifted teacher, who doubled as her social studies teacher, told the class that the highest scorers on some test qualified for enough scholarship money to get them out of Scottsboro if that's what they wanted.

Kids couldn't take the test until they were in high school, but it was a good idea to start preparing now. Deborah hoped there was such a thing and that the teacher knew what she was talking about. She wasn't sure if she could trust her, though, because the teacher was a Democrat and Daddy said Democrats wouldn't have a pot to piss in unless they took it as a government handout. Daddy was very much against handouts.

He was strange, too. Some nights he just ignored her while he ate his dinner, and others he would reign supreme at the table, issuing family decrees and doling out life lessons to her. He was so confident in his tone it was hard to pick out the fact from the opinion, and Mom was no help at all. She just stared blankly at the empty chair at the table. She used to put a plate full of food at Brent's spot until Daddy finally convinced her it was a waste to fill a plate for a boy who couldn't eat, especially since there were starving kids in Africa. All she said was, "There are starving kids right here in Jackson County, Isom." After that, Brent's place was set, but no food was served.

Nonny did not join them for meals, even after Mom got her healed up enough to come upstairs and move into Deborah's childhood bedroom. She helped prepare them and would take a plate to her room. Daddy installed a TV in the room with satellite reception. Nonny ate at her TV tray with sitcoms from the 1960s blaring.

Daddy even offered to take down all the dolls hanging around the walls, but Nonny declined. She glanced at Mom and Deborah and said, "They keep me company." She lived like a ghost among them, rarely engaging the family but being ever-present. The one time Deborah plopped down on her old bed just to check on Nonny, she got shooed away with a, "Get on, gal. Your daddy don't want me a-interfering."

Sometimes, Daddy was nice. He brought her presents, little things like lip gloss or a record or a cute outfit. He always asked her to model the clothes, makeup, and hairstyles she liked to try for him, and she was glad to do it. Finding approval in Daddy's eyes was rewarding, especially when she could make him smile. The items he brought always made her look a little older, feel a little more grown up.

Oddly, though, her books began disappearing from her bookshelf one at a time. At first, Deborah thought she was misplacing them, but when Rebecca no longer sat in its revered spot on the top row, she knew her collection was being pilfered.

184

The stairway to her room was too long and dangerous for Nonny to be squirreling her books away. Daddy gave her gifts, even subscribing to Seventeen magazine in her name, making her something of a romantic expert among her classmates, who were not yet allowed to subscribe to such a mature magazine. She preferred the personality profiles over the gushy stuff, though, because she could answer them different ways and predict the results. That left Mom, who was probably jealous that Daddy didn't give her nice things like he did for his daughter.

Deborah worked all this out in her mind while she walked about the yard and beyond, making broader circles even though darkness came sooner and sooner. Sometimes she just moved out of sight of the house and leaned up against a tree to read. She also thought about the dreams. Her Manderley was not a mansion, not a mountaintop, but a *Mantis*. That's what Renny called her ship and Deborah could see it in dreamscapes with Renny's eyes, feel the warm gulf breeze on her neck across time and space into the Alabama nights, as real as the bark of the tree biting into her back at this very moment.

Nonny held onto the replica as if it were a talisman to ward off Renny's wanderings. She held onto habits and her Bible to keep the dead from rising, but Nonny missed the point. It was interesting how Nonny could be so right and yet so wrong at the same time. Mom fought off the ghost by ignoring her completely, another mistake. Only Deborah was wise enough to discover what the tiny ship held. Only Deborah felt the heady power that came from accepting Renny's presence rather than rejecting it. Even though Renny was her grandmother ageless, Deborah recognized her as a contemporary in both age and spirit, more an older sister than the matriarch of a long line of embittered women.

Mom and Nonny had it all wrong. Renny wasn't wreaking ghastly vengeance on them, hellbent on destroying any hope of happiness in their lives. She was protecting them, just like she protected Deborah from that evil babysitter all those years ago

185

and just like she protected Deborah from getting run down by that school bus when Brent met with his tragic accident. She woke Deborah in time to escape the fire that claimed Nonny's house. Renny told her these things in her dreams, skirting around the corners of her conscious mind since the day Deborah opened the tiny ship and breathed in the aged collection of revelations whispered into the hold by Renny herself.

Every time the specter broke into the present, into Deborah's life, had been a time of high emotion when life and death hung in the balance. She was younger and not able to see life as clearly. Confused by the details, she failed to see Renny's helping hand and only saw the aftermath, the death.

Always an excellent reader, Deborah could see through the facades people built around their lives, encasing themselves in diaphanous walls. She learned to tone her perception down like selecting a station on a radio dial because she uncannily identified the root of their motivations. Knowing what motivated people made it easy for her to manipulate them.

It worked with relative simplicity on strangers, especially her teachers, but she couldn't see as clearly with members of her own family. Perhaps the shared blood muddled her perception. She did understand, however, that her mother and grandmother were both motivated by fear. They were different fears, but at their heart was her grandmother ageless, smiling at her in approval. She was learning.

***

Deborah worked her way back toward home, dragging the metal detector in the dirt behind her. She wasn't really supposed to do that, but it gave the tool a well-worn look when most of the time it just rested neglected in the undergrowth. She needed to find some rusty old thing soon, though, so Daddy would see her appreciation and get her something else.

His latest gift to her was a bizarre set of silk pajamas, surely too tiny for her body, but Daddy promised they would fit her just right. It was called lingerie and was very grown up, so grown up that Mom would get upset and take it away from her if she knew about it. He told her she could model it for him when he came upstairs to kiss her goodnight. It would look darling with her other very special gift, which he couldn't wait until Christmas to give her. Daddy got down on one knee like a prince and proffered a small box.

He opened the box to reveal a delicate necklace with a golden heart woven through the chain.

"This is for you, my beautiful Deborah." He used her grown-up name, the one she preferred. "You have my heart."

"Is it expensive?" she asked.

"Ridiculously," he responded as he clasped it around her neck. The heart rested just on her collarbone, offset from the middle by design. It was very becoming.

"May I show it off to Mom and Nonny?"

"Especially. I want you to wear it until you're ready to marry one day. After all, a daddy is a daughter's first true love." He rose and planted a chaste kiss on her cheek.

"Thank you, Daddy. I love it," Deborah responded evenly, for something didn't feel right about this gift. As pretty as it was, the cool gold on her neck made her feel like she was making a deal or some sort of promise, or maybe Daddy was using her to send a hateful message all wrapped up in love. She shook off the feeling and went to broadcast her gift.

"Did you show proper appreciation?" asked Mom, barely glancing at the necklace, but Nonny shook her head and spat on the pink shag rug.

"A father ought not to give his teenage daughter such as that. What have you been about, Deborah?"

"Daddy says I'm to wear it until I marry one day," she responded haughtily to match her grandmother's tone.

"Harrumph," Nonny responded and turned back to her TV.

187

***

She fingered the necklace now as she decided to take the shortcut back home. The light was growing dim, and she was required to be inside and washed up by suppertime. Almost without realizing it, Deborah found herself at the tree where she last met the incarnation of her grandmother ageless. Terrified, she raced to save her brother from a malevolent spirit only to arrive precisely at the moment of his accident. What a fool she had been. What a child. Renny was urging her forward from a nightmare to save Brent, not destroy him. Renny was helping her, not trying to harm her, the harsh words a spur to action.

If Deborah could see through Renny's eyes in her dreams, why not in waking? Could she call Renny to see through her eyes? It stood to reason. Belief in a ghost was not the question. Renny Clemence was just as real as the necklace encircling Deborah's throat. Her mother ignored her and her grandmother girded herself against her. The haint was most decidedly real. Deborah called out her name.

"Renny?" It was a question, tentative. That would never do. Would she respond to such a wimpy call? Of course not. Deborah projected her voice and made a command. "Renny Clemence of *Mantis*!"

A slight breeze caught her attention in the branches of the tree, but it was the smell that gave the spirit away. Deborah breathed in its pungency: earth, rot, gas, death. She willed herself to turn slowly and face her ancestor. This time she would show no fear. "So, you are real."

"As real as you are, Deborah."

34

Renny

Of all the Clemenceau daughters, Deborah was both first and last. She carried the remaining blood within her and unless she bore a daughter to continue the great circle, Renny would at last cease to be. She crossed oceans of time and space, the tides of her daughters ebbing and flowing as they ran the courses of their lives and moved onward to Heaven or Hell as was their lot.

But not Renny. She remained, breathed into life by the blood of her daughters and the perpetuity of her name. Yes, the name evolved over the generations, but once established, it ran true right down the line through Deborah. It was the curse born of her act of betrayal. That turning away reverberated across the years. Don't all daughters betray their mothers? Don't they all cleave to something else until the roles are reversed and it is their turn to watch their own daughter walk away?

So it is in life; so it is in death. Women reflect their mothers. It's more than a name that is carried forward. It's hopes, fears, and secrets shared whether by rite or necessity. Women find some measure of longevity in the relics they pass down to their daughters—be they recipes, stories, or mourning quilts. Like Shakespeare's mirror trick in *Macbeth*, the future is a line of reflections always holding the essence of an image; immortality realized.

This girl, this granddaughter, and she were inexorably connected. She, like none of the daughters before her, ingested the dust of her own breath. In that Pandora's Box, the girl also found the misery of a mother denied those luxuries of passage. God does not smile kindly on those who throw their mothers away and rains damnation on those who toss their daughters aside.

Yet here she faces this unflinching girl, a picture of resolve on wobbling legs. Both set on staring down the other in a sort of looking glass duel. Both determined to grasp whatever emanates from a vision unable to truly die and a child-woman unable to truly live, she the immediate result of a whore and a madman, and she the ultimate product of that union. Both stand besmirched by others' sins and those of their own making, by the things they have done and the things they have left undone, mirror images separated by the elusive mercury of time. "So, you are real," Deborah stated. Renny could have said the same thing.

"Your curiosity will destroy you," Renny replied.

"Like it destroyed you?" Deborah asked.

"You see me here before you. What destruction? I am ever." The girl ignored this proclamation and took a more practical route. She lifted her chin, but Renny could sense the girl's fear swirling dangerously. She swallowed it down, controlled it. The girl sought to control Renny as well.

"I see through your dreams, but they are so old."

"And I yours, but they are so naïve," she retorted. She loved these recognition scenes, could play them over and over, had played them over and over. She didn't reveal herself to all of the daughters, sometimes preferring to act in shadows. She chose whether despair came with an invisible hand or an undeniable blazoning. The prescient ones, and her Deborah was especially prescient, sought vainly to destroy her, to break the hold of blood.

"Why do you hate our family?"

"I am your family, Deborah.

Deborah's eyes suddenly grew wide as she looked through Renny. There was no time to react, no time to run. Samson was in full attack mode. Teeth gnashing, the dog sprang for the ghost

190

and the girl. Renny let out a laugh and covered Deborah who had fallen back against the tree.

The mingling of spirit, the stench of death, and the smell of piss trickling down Deborah's legs maddened Samson. His teeth clamped down on Deborah's arm, and she screeched. The dog clawed her face with his back paw, drawing blood and sending her heart necklace flying as Samson bit at the area above her head where the ghost hovered and teased the dog with her laughing. He ran around the tree barking viciously, snapping at air. Deborah balled herself up as tightly as possible, blood pouring from the abrasion on her face and whimpering.

Out of nowhere, Nonny appeared, screaming as she hurried toward the tree. "You get away from her, you damned bitch!" Nonny was swinging her cane wildly. She caught Samson behind the ear with an uppercut and sent the dog sprawling. It knocked him out of his crazed state, and his haunches went down as he slinked out of range.

"You damn fool child! What the hell are you doing? You're hurt bad. Can you get up? I can't carry you back to the house. C'mon, get up. You must walk. We'll get your mama to call the ambulance when we get home."

Nonny yanked Deborah to her feet.

She was dazed and kept repeating, "He didn't mean it. He didn't mean to hurt me."

"Hush now. The dog's gone now and so is that demon. Take my jacket and wrap it around you. Let's get you home." Nonny guided her along the way. She stooped to scoop up that unholy necklace, momentarily forgotten by Deborah, hiding it in the palm of her craggy hand.

"How did you know to come?"

"The dolls said you needed me and as soon as I stepped outside I followed the stench. You stink of the rot, child."

191

35

Caro

"She's a very lucky young lady," said the emergency room technician. "That dog barely missed her eye. She could have been blinded."

"That damn dog about took her arm off and scarred the hell out of her, and you call her lucky?" Daddy was beside himself. He held possessively to Caro's arm as they stood in the partition, with only blue curtains providing an illusion of privacy.

"She could have been blinded," the technician repeated, "But she'll heal up in time." He left the room.

Isom bent down to stroke his daughter's bandaged head and spoke softly for fear of being overheard. He didn't understand why hospitals didn't offer private rooms exclusively, even in the emergency areas. No one wants strangers listening in on private sufferings. "Don't you worry, Little Debbie, I took care of the damn dog. He'll never attack you again."

"Oh, no, Daddy. You don't understand. What did you do?" Deborah grasped her mother's hand, but she withdrew it and stepped away from the bed.

"Fed him a pack of hamburger and put a bullet in his head. Damn thing never knew what hit him."

Deborah started to cry.

"You don't need to be crying over Samson. You know we can't abide a dog who attacks his own people. You want to squall, then cry over your face. You'll never make cheerleader now. Hell, no man will love you now. You're ruined. Where's my necklace?"

Deborah brought her hand to her throat, her wounded arm already seeping blood through the dressing. She had to endure that tetanus shot Mom threatened after all.

"I had it on, Daddy. Samson must have knocked it off. I'll look for it when we get home."

"You damn well better find it because you sure as hell won't be getting a wedding ring after this," he replied.

"Isom, don't start in on her. She's hurt. She needs to rest and let the medicine work," Mom said. Isom looked hard at her. She would pay for bossing him later, she knew, but for now the attention needed to be turned to Deborah.

"I'll warm up the car," he said and stepped out of their shrouded cubicle.

***

Hours later, Deborah was snoring quietly on the couch, the painkiller lulling her into deep sleep. Caro wanted her close, so she could keep an eye on her. She also wanted a viable excuse for leaving Isom in bed alone in the middle of the night. He was the lightest of sleepers, but the stress of the afternoon caused him to knock back a couple of extra beers and a slug of whiskey from the bar, so he effectively medicated himself into an all-night slumber.

She rose and murmured softly that she was checking on Little Debbie, but instead padded silently down the hallway past Brent's emptied room to Nonny's door. It was ajar, and she slipped inside to crawl in the bed with her mother like she did when she was just a little girl.

"I knew you'd be here before long," Nonny said as she patted Caro's leg.

"She's not going to let Deborah go, is she?" whispered Caro.

"No, child. You know this," responded Nonny.

"You know this," mimicked Little Debbie's crib doll from her vantage point on the wall. From the ceiling fan hung Nonny's

193

little ship. It made indolent arcs on its chain. Inside its dark hold rested a golden necklace, secreted away with Nonny's craggy arthritic hand, her defense against sins known and unknown.

Epilogue

The indelible mark of a mother's influence over her child extends well beyond the mother's lifetime, woven with that of her mother and her mother before her. Just as resemblance can be passed down genetically, proclivities can be passed down as organically as a family name. Complex as an umbilical cord, sustaining or choking, maternal love is both born and borne. A mother may lay down her life for her son, but the relationship with her daughter runs much deeper than a mere lifetime. That cord, invisible though it may be, connects the mother and daughter, binds them together with the lore of the mothers and daughters before them and to come. The earthy wisdom of habit and pattern makes smooth the path for the voices of the past and present—mother to daughter to mother to daughter—manifest, for those perceptive enough to hear that still small sound. A mother's greatest fear and greatest hope for her daughter, after all, is synonymous: may she fly on her own inexorable strength.

About the Author

Ghost stories were as much a part of growing up as music lessons in Rocky Porch Moore's secluded childhood home atop July Mountain. Today, she keeps the legacies of her mother and grandmothers alive for her own daughters through their recipes, beautiful handmade quilts, and family lore.

Moore's debut novel *Clemenceau's Daughters* was recognized as a Readers' Favorite Five Star Book. The novel also garnered awards in three categories at the Florida Authors and Publishers Association President's Awards, including a gold medal for horror. *Clemenceau's Daughters* claimed honorable mention for general fiction at the Readers' Favorite International Book Awards.

Rocky lives on a farm in Foley, Alabama with her husband of twenty-seven years, their teen daughters, and a passel of farm critters. She enjoys reading, blogging, biking, and cooking. You can follow her adventures at www.rockyporchmoore.com.

Discussion Questions for Book Clubs

1. The names of characters shift over the course of the book, particularly for Deborah and Renny. What is the significance of these shifts, and what do they reveal about the developing psyche of the characters?
2. How does Brent's death affect the family dynamic? For whom was sending Deborah to live with her grandmother beneficial? For whom was it detrimental?
3. What does it mean to be able to "read" people? Is this ability a family trait, or is it nurtured?
4. What role does egocentrism play in this novel?
5. What role does religion play in the novel? How are Nonny, Caro, and Cecille similar in their beliefs? How are they different?
6. Why are Deborah and Renny so strongly linked? In what ways are their experiences parallel?
7. Is Isom a modern Clemenceau? Why or why not?
8. The novel explores multiple comic moments at what may be considered inappropriate times. Choose one such moment and explain what it reveals about a character and his/her motivations.
9. What does the immolation of the mourning quilt symbolize?
10. Which character is more sympathetic: Isom or Captain Bonneval? Caro or Cecille? Mrs. Garlan or Randall? Deborah or Renny?